18'

IDA JESSEN

A Change of Time

Translated from the Danish
by Martin Aitken

archipelago books

Copyright © Ida Jessen, 2015
Originally published as *En ny tid* by Gyldendal, Copenhagen
English language translation © Martin Aitken, 2019

First Archipelago Books Edition, 2019

Library of Congress Cataloging-in-Publication Data

Names: Jessen, Ida, 1964- author. | Aitken, Martin, translator.
Title: A change of time / Ida Jessen ; translated from the Danish
by Martin Aitken. Other titles: *En ny Tid*. English
Description: First Archipelago Books edition. | Brooklyn, NY :
Archipelago Books, 2019.
Identifiers: LCCN 2018030077 | ISBN 9781939810175 (pbk.)
Classification: LCC PT8176.2.E7977 N913 2019 | DDC 839.813/8--dc23
LC record available at https://lccn.loc.gov/2018030077

Archipelago Books
232 3rd Street #A111
Brooklyn, NY 11215
www.archipelagobooks.org

Distributed by Penguin Random House
www.penguinrandomhouse.com

Cover art: Vilhelm Hammershøi

This book was made possible by the New York State Council on the Arts with the
support of Governor Andrew M. Cuomo and the New York State Legislature.

Archipelago Books also gratefully acknowledges the generous support of the
New York City Department of Cultural Affairs, the National Endowment for the Arts,
Lannan Foundation, the Carl Lesnor Family Foundation, the Danish Arts Foundation,
and the Nimick Forbesway Foundation.

PRINTED IN CANADA

A Change of Time

Diary of L. Høy
Schoolteacher

January 3, 1904

I am on my way now. Everything is packed. I haven't even the time to write this. I shall continue later.

May 19, 1905

Yesterday I received a visit —

October 8, 1927, Thyregod

There has been so much tidying up in the house these last few days I thought I would see if I too might have something to put away and conceal. But what could it be? And from whom? I went upstairs nevertheless, and in the cupboard in the spare room, at the bottom of an old munitions box, I found this diary. I have no recollection of it.

The weather is odd for October. Twelve degrees Celsius, the thermometer says, and the air is still and damp. The trains can be heard quite clearly.

In the same box I found a paraffin lamp with a brass base, which I do remember, and seeing it again made me feel rather glad. It was as black as coal. I polished it and put it in the window facing the garden. At first I wanted it to be seen from the road, but I changed my mind. It casts a somewhat furtive light. A secret friend. That would at least be one thing to conceal.

It is lit now.

Evening.

There is the strangest lull. I cannot comprehend it. Perhaps it has something to do with the lamp, its milky, round globe a full moon held forth by an invisible hand. Again, the train can be heard all the way from Kokborg, ten minutes of trundling and then the long pull in to the station, the whistle of the guard, doors slamming shut. The day has been mild and dank. The air, even now in darkness, grey with moisture. But it does not rain.

People come to see me. I am gladdened by their visits, yet also by their leaving. They bring cakes so that I might not be burdened by the baking, and today they offered to make coffee themselves on learning that Line was on her day off. The butcher Schnedler's wife brought a whole boiled tongue with her, and returning home from a late afternoon walk I discovered a dozen eggs on the doorstep.

I look at my hand and urge it sternly to raise itself and pick up the cup while the tea is still hot. But it will not, and does not.

I tidied the spare room with the thought of sleeping there

now. The two beds in the bedroom make me shiver. The head and footboards are mahogany and boxlike, and remind me of marital custom in India, where it is said the widow is burned on the pyre along with her dead husband.

I lit the fire, too. To make it more like a home.

The room is never used. The curtains are hardly more than a pleated ribbon at the upper windows. In the sills lay fat, dust-covered flies that had once buzzed and spun while perishing slowly, and no sooner does one think them dead than they start dying all over again. I swept them all onto a newspaper and tossed it into the blazing peat. I cleaned the windows too, and aired the room and scrubbed the floor. I bundled the mat down to the soggy garden and draped it over a bush. The room is now clean and fresh, and yet I do not wish to return to it. It is an unfamiliar place. A sharp smell of soap.

I think I shall sit a while longer.

October 10

This strange gravity, the peculiar peace that descends in the evenings when the houses turn inwards and people retire to bed. I have begun to expect it, to look forward. It requires so very little. That I am alone, and that darkness has fallen. That I light the lamp. That I gaze into its flame. I do not think of day. And yet that is untrue. If I am congealed fat, blood pulses nonetheless in my depths.

But the day wails. I cannot be home in the daytime. I go about in great shawls, the cold creeps in at my wrists. My hands are blue! I walked to the station and boarded the train. Stationmaster Haldbo ushered me aboard and said: "We must hope. We hope and pray to God." He helped me inside to be seated before blowing the whistle. Human kindness is my nourishment, and my fatigue. Why is it not sufficient? I have more than most.

My house lies above the hill. It is large and made of red brick, with a red tiled roof and a white rendered cornice, built eight years ago by Iversen, the town's builder. Between the house and the station lies the pasture belonging to Vester

Farm, the grass dappled with cowpats and molehills. But the cows are inside now. And beneath the house, at the bottom of the hill, begins the town, with Johannes's cobbler's shop, the dairy, the co-operative society, the grocer Hansen's big red premises, the grocer Rosenstand's slightly smaller ones. Borgergade is the high street, and it grows ever longer. When I arrived here twenty years ago the town barely existed. Is it conceivable that it will continue to grow? The Tradesmen's Association and its members are certainly being kept in business. What will the place be like in fifty years? A hundred?

I took the 11:32 to Give. The journey passed quickly, a mere three quarters of an hour and I was at the hospital. "He's sleeping," said the nurse. "But do sit down. You'll be hungry. Let me get you something."

"Thank you," I said. "But I had a bite before the train."

She looked at me, then said: "It's important to eat, you must remember."

I sat down on a chair by the bed and placed my hand on his on top of the cover. It was icy cold. His finely curved nails had yellowed, the tips of his fingers were shiny. He would be unable to submit a fingerprint now, his distinctive features all receding, his eyes shrunk back, sunken in their sockets, lids closed to cover them, mouth and cheeks collapsed into his face. His gentle flesh is gone, though heaven knows there was precious little to begin with.

I put his hand under the cover, only to retrieve it again some moments later to give it warmth, taking it in both my own, which were just as cold, and burying them all in the shawl.

The hour is late. A short while ago I stood outside on the front step. The street lights are extinguished now, and the lamp on the station's gable end. If a person knew no better, they might think there were no streets at all, no houses, no people, no dogs. No fields ploughed, no hen coops, no sheds. One might think it all reclaimed by the heath. Or that we had never been here.

October 11

Last evening, while standing on the step and thinking myself to be in the middle of nowhere, the air was still. But two hours later I awoke at the sound of the window rattling, and all day the wind has been getting up. The stationmaster Haldbo greeted me with his hand firmly on his hat to prevent it blowing away. At that time, late morning, it was as if the horizon were cut in two in the horizontal. Blazing yellow below, darkness above. "Can this weather not be driven away?" he shouted through the gusts, helping me into the carriage with a hand at my elbow.

Nurse Svendsen met me in the corridor. "Oh, it's a shame you weren't here an hour ago," she said. "He's been awake all morning. He was being silly with me."

She didn't recall in what way exactly. But it was to do with him asking her to find him a pen and paper. He had lain there a while with the pen in his hand. "He's quite exhausted now," she said, ushering me into the room. She measured his pulse, then smoothed the covers. "You must be hungry," she said.

"Do you want me to get you something?" I sat down on the chair. "Yes, please."

A moment later she returned with a cup of tea and a cheese sandwich.

The chair. I took his cold hand in mine, and in a short time mine was cold too. When after a while I let go, I saw his index finger curl into the cover and straighten again. It repeated.

"Are you there?" I asked.

There was no reply.

I felt upset for having let go too soon and by it having occurred on the cover and not in my hand.

I went out to find Nurse Svendsen and asked for pen and paper, thinking that if he wanted to write then I would do so too. I would leave him a letter.

What did I put?

It took me some time, though it contained little of substance. It was nearly four o'clock by the time I was finished. I asked for an envelope and stood the letter by the bedside lamp, instructing Nurse Svendsen to give it to him when he woke up. I just had time to catch the train home. It had started to rain. The wind buffeted the carriages and the window steamed up as soon as I entered in my wet clothes. I was the only passenger in the compartment between Give and

Thyregod. The hedgerows looked like they were doubled-up in the fields.

I arrived home to the cold smell of cigar that lingers in the living room, and the peat box was empty. Line is still off. I have told her not to give it a thought and that I would let her know when to come back. She has returned to her mother in Uhe.

I lugged more peat up from the cellar and hurried to light the fire. Our peat comes from a bog at Vorslunde now and has less sand in it than our own. Porridge for dinner. I put *Winterreise* on the gramophone and removed it again almost immediately. Only when the place is completely quiet am I comfortable. As if this were how one kept one's equilibrium.

The lamp is in the window.

What did I put? I thought so hard about it that I can recall nothing but my efforts to think of something appropriate. If one is offered a single chance to speak one's mind, what does one choose to say? Whatever one says, the exact opposite can always be said too, and with equal justification.

Only then do I realize that the gale has subsided. I go out onto the step. The street lights have been put out, the station lamp too. Not a dog or a crow to be heard. A silence greater than silence. The town is weary, flogged by wind.

October 12

The letter was gone from the bedside table when I arrived at the hospital today. Nurse Svendsen came in with a cheese sandwich and a cup of tea and was full of talk about autumn and winter, with which she has difficulty coping, being from milder climes on Fyn. "Oh, but you're from Ryslinge," she remembered all of a sudden. "You'll know all about it, then. Does a person ever get used to it?" I said she would.

She stood and was chatty. It made me glad, and I was reluctant to let her go.

"Did he get my letter?" I eventually got around to asking. Yes, he did, she told me. He had woken up just after I left yesterday, and she had given it to him straight away. To think, he had been playing around with her again, wriggling his eyebrows and making her laugh. But even that wears him out, she said. "Anyway, mustn't stand here chatting."

The room was silent when she left.

I ate the sandwich and drank the tea, which was good and strong and hot.

His face was unaltered since yesterday, the orbs of his eyes covered by the deathly membranes of his eyelids. Always, I have wanted to look into his blue eyes. The fire of that urge burns still, though I have long since become an old wife. How I have yearned for its flame to be extinguished. For no embers to remain. Nothing that might ever reignite. Consigned to the ash pan.

"Look," I said out loud. "Look what I've brought you." I held a hand up in front of his face, trying to fool him.

I sat down. A short time later, I said: "Open your eyes."

He didn't. And yet I had the feeling he was awake.

October 13

Still it rains, and the wind has returned. This morning saw fifty minutes of sulphurous yellow sun on the horizon. The colors in the garden changed. Suddenly it was as if an illumination welled up from the ground and the redcurrant bushes were dripping with moisture. The light played in each droplet. I wanted to go for a walk, but when I emerged onto the step in my coat, umbrella in hand, I saw Carl Carlsen come bicycling with his camera on a strap across his shoulder. It turned out he wanted to see me. He had apples with him from home. I invited him in, but he would venture no further than the hall. He is a grown man now. Ages can pass without me seeing him. And this time I realized he is indeed what people here say he is: odd. Whenever I have heard it said, I have always called it nonsense and thought to myself it was because they didn't understand him.

It is hard to say what it is. He handed me the apples and told me they were Belle de Boskoop, Maglemer, and Nonnetit Bastard. He uttered these peculiar names in the same way he might have said eating apples and cooking apples.

I was reminded of a time he came to collect eggs from us because he wanted bantams to keep and ours were bantam eggs. On that occasion he had stood at the counter in the scullery and placed the eggs in a basket. He was perhaps twelve years old. He looked at me and asked in all earnestness if the eggs were fertilized. For some reason I was moved by the situation and have never forgotten it. Perhaps it was his absorption in the matter. The innocence of a boy's neck. I felt the urge to place my hand upon it. It was covered in the fairest down.

His figure has become rather awkward, as though he were aged. He is not particularly tall, though quite handsome, albeit perhaps not in a way for which a girl might fall. He resembles his father and mother at the same time. He did not look at me as we stood there in the hall. My impression was not that he felt uncomfortable, but perhaps he did not feel comfortable either. I asked if he took photos often, and he said he did. I asked what kind of pictures he took, and he said he photographed houses and people, landscapes, animals, and machines. "You must come by one day and show me," I said. He promised he would. "I imagine you help out at home when you're not taking photographs?" I said, and he nodded. I asked about his sisters, Dagmar and Inge, and he told me they were at Vallekilde, where they were learning sign language and braille. "It's good, because then Dagmar will be able to talk to Inge," he explained.

"How marvelous," I said. "I'm very pleased to hear it."

"I am, too," he said.

There is a goodness in him. It must be enticed, but will then show itself willingly. Otherwise, it will remain inside.

Nurse Svendsen received me in the corridor. She never speaks of improvement, though imparts small tokens to raise hope. Today she told me she had persuaded him to eat by cutting his bread into soldiers. He had eaten three and had drunk a glass of milk besides. She spoke in a mawkish, prideful manner, as if talking about her own child. Ostensibly it was to please me, only she was pleasing herself. She has no idea what it would mean if that compulsion were ever truly to be acted upon. The way things are now, she will always be able to pride herself on having taken care of him until the last, and would surely be able to repeat every word he has uttered. In her dotage she might write a piece about his deathbed for the Vejle County Year Book. She said he was asleep.

I drew up the chair and sat down at the bed, and put my hand on his.

A twitch passed over his closed eyelids. He did not move. But he was awake.

I tried to think of something to tell him. Carl's visit, the peat, the eggs on the step, the wind, the lamp. *Winterreise*, that I had been unable to listen to, because it was not he who had put it on, bending over the gramophone with his back to the room, carefully putting the needle down, and then, once it had found its groove, abruptly straightening up to remain standing there, brimming with anticipation, immersed in something that was of no one else's concern, until the first tones struck up and he raised his arms and began to conduct. So delightful. But the thought unraveled.

October 14

"How fortunate that you should come now," said Nurse Svendsen. "Here, let me take your coat. He's awake. He's just eaten. Four slurps of broth, full of vitamins. Hurry along. He's so looking forward to seeing you."

She beamed. I handed her my soaking wet coat and hurried along to his room. The light inside was dim. A small lamp on the bedside table had been turned on. He lay with his arm over his eyes.

"Does the light bother you?" I asked.

"Yes," he said.

I turned it off. It would have been natural to have kissed him then, but his arm was in the way and I was unable to reach his face. I could not kiss his hand either, since the position in which it dangled at his cheek in respect of the pillow precluded any approach.

"It's raining," I said.

"So I hear."

"It's a lovely sound."

"Hmm."

"A lot of people have been asking about you."

"Hmm."

I drew the chair up to the bed and sat down.

"It's been such a long time since we spoke," I said. "The house feels empty."

"Line will be looking after you, I'm sure."

"I've given her some time off."

His hand twitched ever so slightly. "It's your own fault then."

"Yes."

Renewed silence.

"Is there anything you want?"

"No, thank you."

"Mette Svendsen says you've had some broth."

He said nothing.

"She was so happy you'd eaten."

"She's a good nurse."

"Yes, she is."

I found a handkerchief in my bag and blew my nose as quietly as I could.

He moved his arm away from his face and placed his hand palm upwards on the cover. I leaned forward and took it in mine.

"I hear you've been writing," I said.

"Yes, a little."

His hand lay so still in mine.

"I wrote to you too," I said.

He gave my hand a faint squeeze.

"Were you able to read it?"

"Yes."

Behind me, the weather washed down the panes. Sudden lashing bursts, followed by softer precipitation. When we were small, Agnete and I thought that gentle rain sounded like the almspeople eating their porridge in the dining room. A quiet slurping, courteous. Nurse Svendsen came tiptoeing with tea and a cheese sandwich for me. She paused in the doorway, but I waved her in.

"Sorry, I didn't mean to disturb," she whispered.

"It's quite all right, he's gone back to sleep," I replied.

"Perhaps he'll wake up again shortly."

He was still asleep when it was time for me to go. The train leaves at 17:03. For a brief moment, I thought I might take a room at the hotel. I could easily have done so, but I did not. I suppose I thought it unnecessary. I could have been sitting with him now. I am sure he must have woken up again. Perhaps he is awake at this moment. Mette Svendsen will tell me tomorrow, beaming with the news. She *is* a good nurse. Attentive to the needs of others. Nothing ever too paltry as not to awaken her enthusiasm and interest. One should be grateful indeed. He reminded me, and indeed I was.

What will I do when he is no longer here? Who will then remind me of what I am to think? Who will keep me in place?

I shall have to find my own place.

I can almost hear his voice: "Poppycock," it says. Meaning: Don't be so conceited, woman.

Time for bed.

I did not in fact sleep at all last night. It has been a long time since I have lain awake in such manner, utterly awake. Naturally, I thought about Vigand, and the fact that I have never known anyone quite like him. The pillow was hard, and the mattress was hard, and yet I told myself that if only I lay still instead of tossing and turning I would at least find some measure of rest.

During his time here he has done so much good it would defy most any audit. No one can say of him that he is snobbish and superior, nor that he tends his own interests. He has no idea what "own interests" even means. There is something impervious about him that some people I am sure find objectionable, but which I think is innocence. With the fierce contempt for death that only a young man can possess, he came here of all places and became district physician for fourteen impoverished and far-flung parishes, and that contempt has never left him, though time has passed and others in his position would have grown rather more complacent. There had never been a doctor here before he came, and in the first twenty-four years he was on his own. No part of the country is like Vejle's western tracts. It was hardly even on the map then.

I have heard that as recently as in 1870, ninety per cent of Thyregod parish was heathland, and I am sure it is true, for what I remember best from when I first arrived here are the sandy roads. Sand as fine as any beach, sand like flour. The very moment one became confident in stride, one could step into a hole. It was as if the sand were a thing alive, shrinking back suddenly at an encroaching foot, with not a measure of firm ground beneath. Johan Nielsen, who carried goods between Give Station and Thyregod, turned his cart over almost daily. I know the children found sport in recovering wares from the ditches, having surprised them once at break when they were standing in a huddle behind the building with the publican's Oscar in the middle. All through the day I had been unable to fathom what they were up to at recess. When I came upon them they fell silent and shuffled closer together with their backs towards me. Their hands were clutching bars of violet soap. Oscar had discovered a whole box and hidden it away in the boys' washroom. Not a single bar had they unwrapped, but passed them instead from hand to hand with the utmost reverence. Later, I wondered what they would have done had it been sweets they had found. Would they have been quite as steadfast? I think so. Eventually, I am sure they would have succumbed, though only after a very long time. I sent Oscar to the grocer Hansen with the soap, since his name was on the box. He came back in the middle of the next lesson, cheeks slapped fiery red, bristling.

And the same children it was, with Oscar Vestergaard, Janus Vestergaard, and Jens Thiis Hansen the most prominent among them, who saw Vigand be thrown from the cart on his way out to Hedebjerg Farm. Having no driver of his own at the time he had to make do with whatever transport he could find. Most had only rigid work carts, for which reason he had his own spring seat that could be fitted to the box. Perhaps it had not been properly secured, or perhaps the straps were poor. At any rate, he and the seat were catapulted far into the field when the cart ran into a hole, and the boys came back after recess fizzing with excitement and gossip. "*T'dowtor, ee wor scrabblin' aboot in t'muck wee's backside in t'wind. Yee shud'v hordim cuss,*" they cried. "*Wot's tha bluddi plaen' at, Jens Madsen? If tha's garn dee'ell, yee c'n let me's off forst!*" Their little voices were a shrill and gleeful chatter. It was at that time the consumption was rife in the district and I did not care at all to hear them speak of the doctor as if he were a poor simpleton whose misfortune they could crow about. Such manners derive not merely from the children themselves, but also from the way matters are talked about in their homes. We had yet to become acquainted. I hardly think he had cast an eye on me. I told them that Dr. Bagge saved lives, and that next time it might be their father's or mother's. I was so angry it gave them quite a fright. I think it made them unsure of my judgement. As I recall, I punished them with detention. And a nasty composition for homework. Probably other things besides. The three of them.

Now, however, it strikes me that Vigand would most likely have been amused if he could have heard them. The way they clucked and squawked, like a brood of hens. And the notion of poking fun at people behind their backs would certainly have appealed to him.

His breathing was different today. Normally it is without resistance, but not today. It was as if he were having to scrape about at the bottom of his chest. I called Mette Svendsen in. "He's sounded like that since you left yesterday," she said.

"What does Dr. Eriksen say?" I asked.

Mette Svendsen patted my hand.

"What does he say?" I asked.

"It may be a long while yet," she said. "He can pick up, and he can fall back."

"How much is a long while?" I asked.

"He's not in pain, that's the main thing," she said.

"How can we be sure?"

"We make sure."

So his sleep was drug-induced. I wondered what had happened after I had gone the day before. Had he complained? Did he make it clear to them that he was in pain? And could he not bring himself to do so while I had been there at his side?

When she was gone, I leaned across the bed. He was bony and unyielding beneath the cover, and his breathing became a groan. I straightened up again with a jolt and stared at him.

"Vigand!" I said.

After I left him, the notion of getting on the train and returning home to the cold house seemed inconceivable. There would be a fire to light and food to cook. I couldn't do it.

I walked along the street. I had stayed behind too long. It was late and I would have to walk briskly if I was going to catch the train. But I ambled, and dwelled on the illuminated windows. I have always been fond of walking in darkness and seeing windows lit up, making plain that people have a home and a place in which they belong. I am drawn by it. But it is not always a comfort, nor always a joy. It may happen on occasion that one considers such lights in the knowledge that the life and joy and warmth one sees is for others. That is not for me. I dawdled.

There were carriages and motor cars outside the hotel, clearly there was a function of some sort. The windows shimmered, and the insides of the panes were thick with condensation.

My feet went up the steps of their own accord, without my will. I asked for a room. I have no idea what expression I was wearing, but Fru Lorentzen, who normally chattered unceasingly, ushered me earnestly upstairs.

As soon as she was gone, I lay down on the bed with all my clothes on. When a knock came on the door shortly afterwards I did not reply.

"There's some food for you," a boy called out in a bright voice. "I'll leave it on the tray here."

I am not sure how much time had passed before I brought it in. There was a portion of clear soup with thick, gritty meatballs in it and a slice of buttered rye bread, left on the table outside the door. Water and aquavit. I put the tray down next to the bed and fell asleep.

It is a good room I have been given. It is warm. Not just heated up towards evening, but all through the day. Hotel rooms can smell of rot and age, but this one smells of baking from the kitchen. It is adequately furnished: a bed, a table and chair. A washstand with a chamber pot. A mirror. A lamp.

The fat has congealed on the surface of the soup. I skim it off into the chamber pot and eat up everything in the bowl. I eat the rye bread too, and drink the aquavit. And then I lie down on the bed again.

I am so grateful not to be at home in the big red house on the hill. It is not my house. Very soon I shall have to move. But to where? I have not prepared myself for anything. This has all come so much sooner than we had imagined. We have never spoken about it. Our words have always been small. It is how we have lived.

It is how we must die.

I sat up with a jolt. A door opened downstairs in the hall. There was a stamping of boots, voices. Presently, more voices, men and women. Laughter. After some minutes they stopped. Then a scraping of chairs in the function room, until that too died away. Shortly afterwards, there was a knock on my door, and when I got up to see who it was, Fru Lorentzen was standing outside.

"Just wanted to see if you were all right," she said.

"How kind," I said. "And thank you for sending up that soup. It was delicious. Thank you very much."

"It'll do you good, I can assure you. Did you eat up? Let me take your tray."

Leaving, she turned and paused in the doorway: "What I meant to ask was if you'd like to come downstairs tonight? It'll be just the thing for you, I'm certain. Have you seen the poster?"

"No," I said. "What's going on?"

"Johannes V. Jensen, the famous writer. He's come to read for us."

"Oh, but surely I couldn't? Hasn't he already begun?"

"Yes, you can. Of course you can. I'll smuggle you in. I was going to look in for a minute myself. Come on, I'll take you down. It's fifteen øre a ticket, but we won't bother about that."

"No, really," I said.

"I insist," she said. "We'll be quiet as mice."

She whispered on the staircase: "He's brought his wife

with him. They're staying the night here and going on to Vejle in the morning."

> *The forbidding, dismal days*
> *Will never, never leave.*
> *Brooding languid is the haze*
> *No light by man perceived.*
> *Not even storm and snows*
> *The year on us bestows.*
> *From morn to eve a fog*
> *Nature sleeps, the dog.*

A lectern had been brought into the function room and behind it stood the great author himself, gaunt and grey, the lights glittering in his spectacles. I sat down and told myself I must remember everything I saw and heard, but with every sentence, every gesture I tried to impress on my mind, the one preceding it was immediately forgotten. He is not a sparkling speaker. The test I set myself proved that my memory is like a sieve. Everything runs through it. Moreover, forcing myself as I did meant only that I became far too aware to take anything in. He spoke of his myths and of his latest collection of poems, *The Seasons*, but apart from this one verse I cannot recall a jot. It came back to me just now, line by line.

Its rhythm suits the days, which pass and pass. And the evenings too, it seems. But then one becomes unsettled by the final line, as if shaken from a slumber.

He had drawn quite an audience and only a single chair in the middle of the room was free. I had intended to stand in the doorway with Fru Lorentzen, but she nudged me forward and repeatedly urged me inside, and eventually I complied, if only to put an end to her whispering. The author paused in full flow and heads turned. Thankfully, my boots did not creak, and I held my head high, accustomed to such looks, and whereas at home they may prompt me to look down, I must nevertheless often have taken time to reflect and wished I could react differently. So I held my head high and fixed my gaze on the two round lenses behind which his eyes presumably were concealed. I was not impolite. And yet he resumed before I had taken my seat. As if having satisfied himself that it was all right to carry on. But now I'm being snooty, I flatter myself.

The crow-bird's hideous rasp
Is winter's horrid cry

In his voice the gloom enclasped
He angles in the sky.
Grey as the mist he is
The tar of night is his
From land to town a straggler
The raucous haggler.

And then this verse comes to me too. One line follows so surely from the next. I write it down as I recall it, no matter that in the morning I could cross the street to the bookshop and purchase a copy of *The Seasons*. But perhaps it is a book I do not care to own.

On my way up the aisle I glimpsed the audience. Pastor Grell from Thyregod was there with his wife, and the new publican, who conceivably has thoughts of repeating such an evening in Thyregod, though I would think it somewhat unlikely that literature could draw folk from their homes in such a place. S. P. Carlsen was there, and Peter Carlsen, who had Carl with him. There were others too.

As mentioned, I made an effort to listen. When it was over, the author was the first to remove himself. I remained seated until the room had emptied. But just as I thought everyone had gone, he came straight towards me, and although I had had more than half an hour in which to prepare myself, I was quite unprepared.

"Good evening, Fru Bagge," he said.

"Good evening, Peter Carlsen," I said. Then I remembered what I was going to say: "Thank you for the apples," I said.

He lowered his head ever so slightly. "They were Carl's own idea."

"I understand he's been taking lots of photographs," I said.

"Yes, he's rather smitten with his photography. Every krone he earns he spends on it. But his pictures are indeed excellent. And his camera seems to be the very thing."

"He's promised to show them to me."

"Then you can be sure he will."

We stood for a moment. "He's here tonight, as it happens," he said. "He thought he might get a picture of the author."

"You get out a lot, Peter Carlsen."

"There'd be no excuse to miss the man who wrote *Himmerland Tales* and *The Glacier*." He smiled. "What are you smiling at, Fru Bagge?"

"It's nice to hear someone talk in such a way, that's all."

"Like what?"

"That there'd be no excuse. It's so simply put."

"Too simple for one such as yourself, perhaps?" he said softly.

"That's not what I meant. But someone else might have said—"

We had reached the hall and were halted by the general hubbub. People stood putting on their coats and fell more or less silent as we appeared. For once, no one spoke to me, apart from the pastor and his wife, who speak to everyone. Later, it occurred to me that they perhaps found it hard to see me at the hotel with my husband being so poorly in the hospital. There is an uprightness among people in these parts that is near uncompromising and which embarrasses many, both those who nourish it and those who find themselves on its receiving end. I think they would like to relieve themselves of it in certain situations. They did not look unkindly upon me. On her way out, S. P. Carlsen's wife leaned forward and gave me a little pat on the arm as she adjusted her headscarf.

I went into the restaurant to ask for a cup of tea and stood at the counter. Two young girls were busy laying tablecloths, setting the tables for the day after. Their round faces blushed with fatigue. Johannes V. Jensen and his wife were having soup over by one of the windows.

"It's a rich soup, I will say," I heard his wife comment. "Boiled from a good, fatty hen. The meatballs are nicely done too."

"It's half cold." He abandoned his spoon in the bowl with a clatter.

"Yes, I was just about to say. Shall I ask them to heat it up again?"

No reply.

"You know how much good it does you to get something inside your stomach."

"I'm not having any more."

"It's only starters. There's roast pork."

"No, I said."

They fell silent. The great author turned to a newspaper. His wife had put her spoon down too by then, and sat in front of her barely touched soup staring out of the window with a glazed expression. All of a sudden she straightened up and called one of the serving girls over and asked for coffee and two pieces of plum cake with whipped cream, and at that same moment Carl Carlsen appeared.

Often I have seen him slinking around at the fringes, not

because of shyness, but out of a wish not to be disturbed in a pursuit of which others are ignorant. It is easily mistaken for self-consciousness. People feel sorry for him and call out to him on the street if he comes cycling by. They think he can be warmed up and gladdened by company. In larger gatherings, he dashes about so as not to become stuck in one place and is here, there, and everywhere, for he has been well brought up and knows that he must conduct himself among others. I have never found it odder than the urge of others to blather on and on.

He approached Johannes V. Jensen directly with his camera against his stomach, announced his name and put out his hand. There was an authority about him, as if he had come to settle an account or book another reading.

"May I be permitted to take a photograph?" he asked.

Johannes V. Jensen put the newspaper down on the table.

"What newspaper are you from?" he asked.

When it transpired that Carl was not from any newspaper, Johannes V. Jensen lost interest and waved his hand in a gesture of annoyance, but Carl remained unaffected and asked if he might photograph the author's spouse instead. I think Fru Jensen was rather surprised by the suggestion. She smiled hastily and glanced at her husband.

"Do as you wish," he said. "As long as it's away from the table."

She was photographed by the French doors, with ruddy cheeks and her chin raised. But then all of a sudden a shyness came over her. My tea arrived, and I retired upstairs. A short time later, I heard the couple pass in the corridor.

Instead of retiring so swiftly I should have approached Johannes V. Jensen and said something complimentary. It would not have been difficult for me. I have read both *The Fall of the King* and *The Glacier*. It would have given him something else to scorn besides his wife. Scorn cannot be broken and cannot be softened, but merely diverted from those it hurts most, if only temporarily.

> *Stiff his gait on dreary field*
> *As twigs his blackened toes*
> *Beak to frozen kelp for yield*
> *Of shellish scraps exposed.*
> *At naked forest's crown*
> *The band of corpses frown*
> *Trees cold that sway and creak*
> *His asylum, bleak.*

And abruptly this verse appears too, almost quite by itself. Yet I think of Fru Jensen, who laid out offerings in vain. Can one ask a person to show that they love you? Reason, that most faithful onlooker to the tribulations of others, says no.

But what say unreason?

Mark, the crow is canny.

Perhaps I shall sleep tonight. I think of Fru Lorentzen's benevolent eyes. I think of Peter Carlsen, who spoke of his beloved Carl. I very much like that he said *earns* money, not *gets*.

> *But mark, the crow is canny*
> *Ask the crow what he knows —*
> *In flight he turns, and crafty,*
> *Caws his nouse, scarcely slows:*
> Aye, speak of golden years!
> Ha, kra, kra, time but sneers! —
> *And laughing, arrows higher*
> *To cloud, the nigher.*

October 16

"We telephoned all evening from six until ten. The lady from the exchange was up looking for you. Dr. Eriksen even drove to Thyregod to find out where you were. Where were you?"

"At the hotel," I replied. "I took a room at the hotel."

"You mean you were here all along?" she said. "If only we'd known."

"I didn't know myself until the last minute," I said. I had no idea why she was talking to me in such a way.

She led me in to Dr. Eriksen, who stood up and put out his hand. He said Vigand died at half past nine last evening.

Simply died.

October 17

It is evening, I have no idea what the time is. All day people have come to the door with flowers and food. They don't want to come in. Some knock and offer a few words. Others simply put what they have brought on the step and leave it for me to find when I go out, but I have hardly been out at all, apart from cycling up to the rectory to speak with Pastor Grell. I haven't the inclination to look people in the eye, nor not to. I find myself in a state of shame. The word itself shames me as I write.

I was out on the step just before. The hour is so late now that all lights have been extinguished, including those of the sky. No stars are out, no moon over Thyregod. Not the slightest twinkle from Vester Farm's water-logged field. At the foot of the hill lies the sleeping town. I am filled by a mad desire – not to cease to exist, but to be alone. To have no one come. No one look in on me. No kindness, no outstretched hands. What are they supposed to help me with? To realize how grateful I should be for their visits, now that I have no one else in the entire world?

Only the deepest ingratitude do I have to give them in return.

They sense and understand it. And thoughtful as they are, they leave their attentions on the step.

It is a still and overcast sky. There is coldness in it.

For supper this evening I had fried egg and a seasoned sausage with a slice of bread. I had looked forward to it, for it is the kind of food I have often longed for when cooking has seemed to me to be the most horrendous waste of time. I set the table, poured water into the glass and placed the napkin on my knee. But after only a mouthful or two, patience deserted me and I left the table. I spent most of the day pottering about the house, rummaging through drawers and cupboards, only to forget what was in them the moment I turned away. I returned to the same drawers and cupboards several times over. Now the place is a mess, the living rooms, the bedroom, the study, all a terrible mess, but it is not enough.

Nurse Svendsen accompanied me over to the chapel yesterday. "I sat with him last evening," she told me. "I thought someone should keep vigil." She was pale and fatigued. When I asked, she told me she had not been to bed, but had been up all night. I squeezed her hand feebly. She opened the door for me and ushered me in, but did not follow. Candles had been lit around the coffin, and I stared at him. I can no longer recall what he looked like. I recall the candles, and Nurse Svendsen's wearied and reverential expression, and thinking about it now I feel the urge to say: There you are, take his corpse. It's all yours!

I went back to collect his things. Everything had been put in the suitcase. His shaving tackle, his pajamas, his dressing-gown. His fountain pen, toothbush, and underwear. His socks, and the slippers Johannes made for him just after we were married. I stood with them in my hands. Fine, hand-sewn slippers in tan, near-black leather. All packed meticulously by Nurse Svendsen.

"Where's the letter?" I asked. She was in the disposal room.

"What letter?"

"You said he wrote something the other day."

"Oh, you gave me a shock, appearing like that. All his papers are in the side pocket in the suitcase."

"What side pocket? I couldn't find anything."

She went with me back into the empty room, where the bed had been washed down, folded together, and put aside against the wall. She bent down over the suitcase and indicated the side pocket with two fingers. "Here," she said.

The envelope said *Fru Bagge*, the words written in his heavy, slanting hand.

My own letter wasn't there.

I went back to the disposal room. "I can't understand it," I said. "Something seems to be missing." She drew herself upright.

"Everything's there, I'm certain of it."

"I wrote a letter to my husband. It's not there."

"I haven't seen anything," she said, perturbed. "I don't know quite where else it could be."

"What about the bedside cabinet?"

"That was cleaned out some time ago. It would have been found. You're welcome to look, of course."

I looked, in the bedside cabinet and the cupboard too. While I was looking, Dr. Eriksen came in. "Your husband had an agreement with the cremation society," he said. I had no idea, but pretended I did. Afterwards, all I wanted was to go home. It felt like everything was expended. I left as if in a state of disgrace. Anyway, I was in time for the train.

I arrived home to the freezing cold house, where I stumbled on the stairs with the peat box. The bricks spilled onto the cellar floor where they lie still. My dress: draped over a chair in the living room to dry. I made tea and wrapped myself up in blankets, then sat down in front of the tiled stove; it took half an hour for the room to warm up even barely. I lit the range in the kitchen, and the stove in the spare room. Standing in front of the open stove in the living room with a blanket over my shoulders, I read his letter. I reproduce it here while I can still recall the wording:

Everything is agreed with P. Møllergaard and the parish council. You've got three months to find a new home, and there should be enough for somewhere decent. Nothing fancy. You'll have to do without Line. Rose Cottage is vacant. You'll be fine.

VB.

P.S. I've sold the car to Dr. Eriksen.

I bent down and put a brick of peat on the fire. And then the letter. It would not catch to begin with; there was time to change my mind if I wanted, but the thought did not even occur to me.

Yet the fact remains, and I must never forget it, that he has provided for me and made sure that my dignity will not be compromised, unless of course I contrive to do so myself, and that he has made arrangements for me not to be evicted immediately, though naturally the parish council is already on the lookout for a new physician, who shall have to be put up in some dingy room and come and go from his consultations and treat the widow kindly, lift his hat and refrain from enquiring too inquisitively as to her habitational predicament, this new young doctor so eager to make a start, to marry and move into his own home.

A new home may be mine too.

He wrote that Rose Cottage is now vacant. It lies in the western end of the town, on a plot parcelled out from the farm called Herthasminde. Its nearest neighbour is Hedebjerg Farm, and not a lovelier place could be found in all the district. The house itself is of red brick. It is not big. There is a small yard with washing lines and outhouses. A pond where ducks might be kept, and a large garden with wind rushing in its trees. Only in that end of the town are there trees for shelter. We who live up here on the hill are as unfamiliar with shelter as those in the windblown high street below. I have often passed the cottage on my walks, and once, when Vigand asked where I had been, I told him about it, and there must have been something in my voice that he recalled. Vigand remembered such things. One morning, many years ago, I sat studying an advertisement for a dressing gown, while Vigand sat opposite reading the main section. I folded the newspaper around the picture when I stood up. At Christmas a couple of months later, his present to me was the same dressing gown. White with red stripes. To be honest, I had forgotten all about it by then. It was a luxury I had whispered in all privacy one morning, without for a moment imagining there to be even the remotest likelihood. And then there it was before my eyes, the wildest surprise on Christmas Eve, and I sprang up and threw my arms around him. "I believe that was the one you liked," he said. I have it to this day. He often wanted to buy me a new one, and actually did on a couple of occasions. But my favorite is the striped one, the one from the newspaper advertisement, the one from that morning.

He has given me blouses, handbags, jewelry, hats. An umbrella with a varnished handle. Scarves, dresses, and boots. And all of the finest quality, far better than the cheap rubbish I have always bought for myself whenever I have been in need of something. When I met him I possessed neither style nor taste and could be happy for even the most inferior item. I never looked at the quality of the fabric, never noticed if a dress did not fit snugly across the shoulders or if the armhole was spoiled by a fold. Although he taught me to tell the difference between what was good and what was poor, my former habits remained, and on several occasions I came home from the sisters Clemmensen, beaming over a new dress, only for him to send me back with it. Once, the elder sister said to me: "I feel sorry for you, Fru Bagge." Of course, it was herself she felt sorry for, because there she was thinking she had managed to sell me four summer frocks, only for me to come back with them an hour after we had stood in the fitting room in complete agreement, blushing and intimate, having admired the items for their fall and twirl and color, and then our entire conversation had been annulled. As soon as the words left her mouth she must have know they would have consequence. And indeed they did, for after that day I stopped buying their clothes altogether.

Their shop is still on the high street, but has since become a proper boutique with awnings outside and two big windows facing out. They have become stout, the both of them. Spinsters still. They have a weaver's shop too, where they weave in the evenings and teach the young girls of the district. They weave tablecloths, mats, cushions, blankets. A display cabinet hangs on the wall outside with a changing selection of their wares.

One of the first things I did when I got home today was to unpack his suitcase. I put his pajamas and underwear in the laundry bin and resisted the urge I felt to bury my face in them. There are times when one must avoid becoming sentimental and muddling matters. I must do the washing as soon as possible. I put his shaving tackle in the bathroom cupboard: the razor, the soap in its porcelain bowl, the shaving brush. Only then did it occur to me that there was no change of clothes in the suitcase. He was lying in the coffin in his new grey suit, the one Heinesen the tailor had made for him in the spring, in his new trousers, waistcoat, and jacket. That lovely line of black buttons. Had he driven off to the hospital in his best suit the day he admitted himself? There has been no messenger here to ask for any grave clothes, I know it myself, even if I do remember poorly.

Did he drive off dressed for his funeral?

All of a sudden I remember nothing and recall him neither saying goodbye nor leaving.

I have written to Line and informed her I can no longer afford to keep her on. I put it as nicely as I could.

$$\sim$$

Vigand was in every respect of the opinion that life and death were a yoke one had to bear without a sulk. Griping was something he tolerated as little in himself as in others. His motto: "That's life!"

He was known for scolding his patients mercilessly. It was an annoyance to him that they should come with their complaints and ailments, and he had no wish to encourage them to demean themselves further. Could they not bear a predicament with dignity? No one has ever received a visit from Dr. Bagge without being raked over the coals for it, people would say, before our getting married prevented them from saying such things to my face. But I know it not to be true. I always have.

And if he was harsh on others, he was no less so on himself. He never told me he was ill, and I have no idea how long he kept it from me, but I have seen him gulping down pills on several occasions in his consulting room. Then came the vomiting. When in September I eventually aired concern, since by that time he had become visibly thin, it had happened gradually during the course of the summer, and I could not help but pass comment, he played it down. It was nothing, he said, his face grey and limp: "Feeling a bit tired, that's all."

"I've heard you being sick," I said. "And not just once either."

"Perhaps you listen in on me shitting as well?" he barked, suddenly enraged. "Do you want me to keep a record every time I defecate?" I have often wished I could laugh, and I am certain it was what both of us wanted more than anything in our marriage, and that it would have made our life together so very much easier. Perhaps laughter might even have coaxed forth some measure of intimacy, and with it other things of which I have no conception in my present state. But I have never been capable of a quick retort. It is a weakness of mine, perhaps my greatest, and one that I cannot hope to overcome, that I so easily take offense. Not that I ever say as much. No, my offense reveals itself by slowly seeping from my voice, which is otherwise so mild.

He lost his appetite. He continued making his rounds until long into the evenings, but normally he would eat when he came home. That stopped. I sliced cold meat for him and baked little puddings, chopped kale and made grated carrot with whipped cream and sugar to sneak some vitamins inside him. "Your cooking's so bloody bland these days," he said.

"My cooking's the same as it's always been," I told him. He gave me a look. It said: Can you not bear to be criticized?

No, often I could not.

His last days before he was admitted to the hospital were spent in his consulting room, unless he was out on his rounds. His patients were few on the final day. He was required only to make a trip to Dørken, and in the evening he was called out to a birth in Vesterlund. Apart from that he was there all day. I made him coffee. Supper on a tray. But the door was locked and he would not let me in. I put the tray outside the door, and when I collected it again the food had a crust on it. Only the coffee did he take in, expelling the cup back to the sideboard in the corridor again when he was finished. There were wide, angry marks on the cup where his lips had touched, and he had spilled from the pot onto the napkin. He banged about behind the door. Drawers were pulled out and slammed shut, instruments clattered in their bowls. He groaned and remonstrated with himself. His words were single syllables: "No!" and "Clean hands!" I rattled the handle:

"Vigand!" I shouted. "Let me in!"

"I haven't the time!"

"I'll go for help, if you don't let me in."

He did not let me in. I did not fetch help. He knew that the only threats to issue from my mouth were the empty kind. Who could have put Dr. Bagge in his place?

Few indeed. P. Møllergaard. P. Carlsen. In all discretion they could have done so. No one would ever have known.

But Vigand had not lost his mind. In his instance, the mind was the last thing to go after everything else came to a halt. His limbs could wither, but his senses still clung to his wretched body. Even his sleep in those final days at the hospital was canny. I always had the feeling he woke up as soon as I had gone.

I stayed in the house all day without once going out. I don't know how I passed the time. There was an embroidery, I imagine. Domestic matters to be sorted out with Line. Silverware to be polished. That was the day I suggested she take some days off and go home to visit her mother. She left as it was getting dark. I stood on the step and waved to her with a sense of relief, watching her figure grow smaller as she made her way to the station.

I went back inside and closed the door. Sat down in the living room without switching on the light. Then the telephone rang. We have two, one in the consulting room and one in the living room, besides a system of bells throughout the house, including outside, so that any call may be heard even from the garden. I picked up the receiver and heard Vigand's voice, he had already answered, so I put it down again. Shortly afterwards, he was standing in the doorway with his bag in his hand and told me he had been called out to a birth in Vester, and everything was at once returned to normal. He asked for a sandwich and I went out into the kitchen and made him one and opened a bottle of beer. He ate at the oilcloth-covered table in the kitchen, I sat down on the bench and we chatted as if nothing had happened. He said he might be some time and that there was no need to wait up. He patted my hand as he got to his feet, and a few moments later the exhaust spluttered angrily against the coach-house walls as he turned the engine over and reversed out.

A fresh sheet had been drawn over the examination table in the consulting room, the steel table with its array of bowls, stethoscope and other instruments had likewise been covered up. I lifted a corner and saw nothing unusual. Everything else was the same too. The sink with the soap next to it. The shelves with their reference books in alphabetical order. The waste bin, empty. Nothing out of the ordinary.

Two hours later, the time was hardly after seven, the car returned. I heard it approach on the road and waited for it to splutter again in the coach house. But it did not transpire. He went in through the consultation, put his bag down and presumably wrote something in the journal. Shortly afterwards he came into the living room.

"A fine, healthy girl," he said. "Already at the teat when I left."

"And the mother?" I asked.

"Happy and content."

"It must have been very quick."

"She's a fine specimen. Made for childbirth."

"You must be tired," I said.

"Not at all," he said.

"Sit down, I'll bring you a cup of tea."

"There's something I need to do first."

I took it that he still wanted tea and went into the kitchen to light the range, which I had allowed to go out after Line had left. When I looked out of the kitchen window the car had gone. I went to the consulting room and found that he had locked the door. Half an hour later he was back. He went upstairs. I heard his footsteps in the bedroom for a while, and when he came back down into the living room he was wearing his long, grey overcoat that he only ever wore on cold journeys in the car. I had arranged the tea table and lit candles. It was a cozy living room. The candles on the piano were lit too. I had polished the brass holders that same afternoon, and they shone and sparkled. I got up when he came in, but he gestured for me to remain seated.

"How nice you've made everything," he said. He crossed the floor, bent down and kissed the top of my head.

"I must give tea a miss tonight," he said.

"What's the matter, Vigand?"

He put his hand on mine. Both were freezing cold.

"Don't get into a state," he said.

"No," I said.

"Good."

He straightened up.

"Everything's taken care of. You've no need to worry."

"Where are you going?"

"A short stay at the hospital."

I said nothing.

"There are certain things that should not be dealt with at home," he said, and uttered a chortle that was so dry and brief it sounded more like he was clearing his throat. It meant: We shall speak no more of it.

He went out into the hallway and picked up the suitcase he had left there, then put his hat on. I followed him out to the car, which he had left on the road, and held the door for him as he got in.

"I'll come and see you tomorrow," I said.

"See you there, then."

He is dead. He does not exist. He can no longer bend down and place a kiss on my head. No more will he come striding unapproachably through the living room. No more will I sit opposite a raised newspaper at the breakfast table. Never again hear the sound of running water as I pause on the landing. He took cold showers. His meager body must have shivered. Vigorously he would dry himself, dropping the towel on the floor when he was done, then stepping over it with his head lifted to the day, already immersed in things to be done, oblivious to himself. Today I have buried my face in his shirts several times. They smell of him: his fragrance was always of soap and eau de cologne. It was he who taught me to use lavender water in the ironing. How unusual for a man to take an interest in that.

I have rummaged everywhere, apart from the consulting room, which remains locked, and the house is now such a terrible clutter. I have no idea what time it is. It could be night or it could be early morning. I have been searching for something personal. I have been through his armoire in the bedroom, though I know full well what it contains, having always looked after his clothes myself. The drawers of the bureau here in the living room are all pulled open, but nothing in them is his. The junk they accommodate is mine alone: reels of musty-smelling embroidery thread; forgotten letters and postcards from my sister, and from my student days at Ryslinge, a couple from my father and mother when they were still in charge of the poorhouse in Faaborg; playing cards and old teaching materials; and *Forty Tales from the History of the Fatherland.*

I have been through the study. And what did I find? Such tidiness, everything neatly in its place. A pen-wiper, blotting paper, sharpened pencils and fountain pens all ordered in the drawer according to size; writing paper, a rubber thimble to place on the finger when leafing through a book, and on the shelves meters of volumes I have never once seen him read. So forcefully did I slam the drawer shut that everything inside was sent rattling.

I went through his books too, having formerly been in the habit myself of hiding secrets in books I felt sure no one else would ever open. I opened every one, lifting each by the spine and shaking it briskly, letting it drop to the floor, then stepping over it with my gaze already fixed on the next.

But if it is the case that I have burned his only written words to me, then so be it. Let them be burned. I have fallen back on myself. It might be night, it might be morning. No light on the stair. No light on the horizon. No lamp lit in the window. No moon held out in the palm of a hand.

Vigand was a free-thinker and did not attend funerals, not even of patients to whom he had been close. They say he did not even attend his parents' funeral. They died when he was young, of diphtheria in Sønderborg. But how could a district physician in such a far-flung place take time off when there was no one to fill in?

So it was I who attended the funerals. Someone from the house ought to, I considered. I have been to many over the years, and of people we knew well. All have been different. Some unbearably grievous, others cheerful and merry, with excellent refreshments.

I once asked him to go with me so he could see what went on for himself. He said there were things to which a person need not subject himself voluntarily.

I asked him how he thought a funeral should take place.

"Obviously, the corpse must be disposed of immediately," he said. "This objectionable custom people have of laying the deceased out in bed or on the dinner table, kissing and fondling them for days on end, makes the flesh creep. Think of the bacteria, the risk of contagion. No, throw them on the fire or get them in the ground as quickly as possible, I say. Though why there should have to be all that caterwauling in church is beyond me."

I laughed, and he did too. I often did when he talked as if he were clipping people's ears. His opinions were so rigid, and they continued to surprise me, even though they were familiar. But I only laughed when it was someone other than me on the receiving end.

"If I die first, I want a proper funeral," I said.

"Proper?"

"With caterwauling in church."

"All likelihood says you won't. So the rest of us won't have to suffer it."

It turned out he was right. But still I found it odd that he should have taken such care of matters and yet left no instruction as to his funeral, until yesterday when I visited Pastor Grell. He ushered me into the living room, not the study. Fru Grell brought us coffee and biscuits, and remained with us. They spoke to me both. Pastor Grell is a cheerful, ruddy man, and she is a cheerful, ruddy wife. They have no children yet. He paints pictures from the district and writes countryside observations for the *Vejle Gazette*, and is altogether highly interested in local custom and folklore. She has a countermarch loom that occupies one of the rectory's many rooms, takes a keen interest in the garden, and invests much effort in parish work. They are always together wherever they go, and have been able even to remain on a good footing with the Lutheran Mission, despite their both being products of the Folk High School movement, for which reason there was much opposition in mission circles when they applied for the vacancy. But that was four years ago now, which is an age. I doubt anyone gives it a thought anymore.

I wanted to speak to him about the funeral arrangements, but before I got round to it, he said:

"I received a letter from your husband a few weeks ago. I think it best you read it yourself."

He got to his feet and left the room for a moment, and while he was away his wife served me coffee.

Vigand wrote this:

Dear Pastor Grell,

I write to you regarding a matter of which I trust you will make no mention until the appropriate time. I shall presently be deceased, and in that connection I do not doubt that you will receive a visit from my wife wishing to speak of a funeral. I do not wish for any such occasion and have therefore arranged with Dr. Eriksen that my body be removed for immediate cremation. In the event that she is distraught, by all means arrange a memorial service to dry her eyes. However, no prayers and no fairy music.

Kindest regards,
Vigand Bagge.

It was dated August 28.

I handed the letter back, and Fru Grell placed a hand on my shoulder.

"Should I not have shown it to you?" the pastor asked.

"Yes," I said to the contrary, partly because he seemed already to have put the word in my mouth, and partly because he was doing his best. It wasn't his fault. But I had never before known Vigand to be quite so cruel.

And then there was the date.

It strikes me now that it was perhaps not me he was seeking to offend, but Pastor Grell, as if he wished to shock him by being so despicably frivolous, now that he had such a strong card to play as his impending death. But Vigand was never so naive. He must have known he would be killing two birds with one stone.

"You needn't make any decision today," said Fru Grell. "A memorial service can be held at any time."

"But there should be one," I said.

"Agreed," said the pastor.

"We can dispense with any fairy music," I said.

"Of course. We can make do with a eulogy and a hymn. And I can read from Ecclesiastes, chapter three."

"That's what I was thinking too," I said. "And I'd like it to be soon."

"So very understandable," said his wife.

Today, over the telephone, we have agreed on the twenty-fifth. In a week's time. His urn will have arrived by then. To be interred in the churchyard.

They followed me out into the driveway when I left.

Vigand was with all his heart of the conviction that one should not be a nuisance, and he could be rudely offensive in order to avoid it. Such an idea is of course in every respect honorable, and yet one may ask whether the right to be a nuisance ought not to be a human right? What if we were to eradicate every nuisance? Who would then be left?

Moreover, I have wished more than anything else that he would make a nuisance of himself to me.

Not that he never did. He *was* a nuisance. Just not in a way I could understand. A man who needed my help, his nuisance I would have understood. But perhaps then it would not have been a nuisance at all. I have never thought of it like that before.

Nevertheless, I am none the wiser.

Ever since I was at the rectory three days ago I have felt like I left a black mark on that cheerful young man. Perhaps he felt the same about me. At any rate, he and his wife were loath to let me go in the driveway that day. He stood there all astutter, glancing at his wife as if they had agreed on the matter beforehand, but had now fallen into doubt.

"One becomes absorbed in the district," he said. "In the countryside, as well as in the people who live here. Occasionally, one hears something that makes an impression, and then . . ." His words trailed away. "I have much pleasure in speaking with Peter Carlsen now and again. I coaxed him into writing down something he told me. I should like to show it to you. I think it might be of interest, and perhaps you will also be gladdened by it."

His wife placed a hand on his arm and he paused.

"I cannot think that Peter Carlsen would have anything against me showing it to you . . . Would you care to see it? It's only a few pages."

I told him I would like to very much, and he scurried away over the cobbles, returning a moment later with some folded sheets of paper held out in front of him. "Is it all right like this? Or should I find an envelope?"

"An envelope would be suitable, Hans," said his wife.

"You'll find he refers to himself simply as *the man*," Grell said. "I'm not sure why. Perhaps he found it easier that way."

His wife went inside to get an envelope.

I read the Peter Carlsen's account that same afternoon at

home in the unheated living room and returned it when I stopped by the rectory today. I had nothing to say when I handed it back, and Grell was embarrassed. He had wished only to make me happy, and yet there I stood unable to muster a single word of compliment.

"Yes," he said. "There we have a most telling testimony to how excellent a physician your husband was, Fru Bagge. How splendid a man."

"Indeed," I said. "How true."

"But of course you knew as much already. It was interfering of me."

"Not at all," I said. "It was kind of you."

And that was true as well.

He asked me inside, and apologized immediately for his wife not being at home. I declined politely. But I did not go home.

I had not been out all day. From the rectory I cycled up past Knudsen's farm. The sky was big and grey. There were crows in the fields, oddly silent.

Nature is silent at the moment, at least when the wind is still.

I carried on through Egeskov wood, and when I emerged and could see the garden at Hedebjerg Farm, I turned down the lane and cycled homewards past Rose Cottage, which indeed stood empty. The apples have not been plucked this year, and the pond was overgrown.

Let us peep into a home, for it is good to see what such a place looked like so long ago. It is a humble home, like most at that time. The man and the wife were young folk, the man's elderly mother had withdrawn from the hardest work and lived now with them. It was the man's childhood home. The farm had been handed on to them upon their marriage. The man had proceeded with pluck and great expectations, having remained at home and helped his mother for eleven years before the deeds to the farm became his. And indeed he made progress, but in his plans it was only the beginning. He felt happiness to be with his young wife and their little boy, Carl, who was six months old, and also his aging mother, of whom they were so fond. The future seemed so very bright for them. True, there remained much to be improved. The soil was bare and exhausted. As yet there was no windbreak, though sapling trees and hedgerows had been planted in the fields and garden. And it was plain to see for anyone that the worst was over.

But then he came down with a cold in the winter, and a dreadful cough that would not go away. When he retired in the evenings, the bed would shake with his coughing, and his mother endeavored to help him with all manner of household remedies, but to no avail. She began to talk of him having to see the doctor.

By April his cough had yet to recede, and his fatigue escalated. One day that month they were particularly busy. A new cement floor was to be laid in the scullery, the work had occupied him since early morning. The cement was lumpy and had to be sieved. The air was filled with dust, and he coughed even more. An unease came over him, for there was so much to be done.

After midday he tilled with a plough he had borrowed. When he was finished, he took it back. Then his coughing took a grip, a shiver of cold passed through him, and he quickened the horse; he needed to get home, for there was so much to be done before evening. Late in the afternoon his mother said: 'You don't look well.'

'I'm not, but when the work is done I shall go to bed.' One of the horses needed scrubbing and its hind leg rubbed with ointment, and because it was such a headstrong beast he had to do it himself, and the pigs were still to be fed as well. He went out into the stable and began with the horse, which pulled its leg away; he became angry with it and took hold again. But then the cough came over him, and his mouth filled with blood. Again he shivered with cold, though his body was burning hot.

He hastened to the pigs. A litter of piglets had broken in to the big sow's sty and she was furious. He stepped in to separate them and the sow mistook him for one of the young she had decided to teach a lesson; his leg bore the brunt, and he could hardly stand, never mind walk. But eventually the work was done and he could go inside.

As he stood washing himself, the cough gripped him again and the blood welled in his mouth, and then once more the singular shivers of cold and sense of fatigue. With unsettled thoughts he went to bed. His young wife came with hot drinks and doted on him. But then again the cough returned and shook him as never before. Blood rose in his mouth for the third time. And yet it grew worse, it was as if his insides were boiling over and spilling from his mouth. The chamber pot filled with blood. It was pale red and looked like froth. Consternation ensued. His brother, Søren Peter, who had come home to help with the scullery floor, mounted his bicycle and pedalled to fetch the doctor, for the telephone had yet to come. At Dørken, the bicycle broke down and Søren Peter ran to the nearest farm and borrowed a horse. Between ten and eleven o'clock that night, the doctor arrived from Give.

'We need your husband to sit up straight,' the doctor said to the young wife after having listened to the man's chest, 'so that I can listen to his lungs from the back.' Turning to the man, who was surprised by his words, he said: 'I want you to remain quite calm.' 'Am I really that ill? You handle me like a small child,' the man said. The examination was concluded, and the doctor gave the young wife his strict instructions: 'Your husband must lie on his back. He must not turn over in the bed. You must not lift him, nor change his sheets. No one is to disturb him, and no one is allowed inside this chamber. If anyone should come to the farm smoking tobacco, send them away. You must watch over him so that you may be at hand should he suffer further attack. One thing is very important, and that is that a window remain open in the chamber day and night so that the air can be as fresh and clean as possible.' The doctor went into the parlor, where the grandmother sat with the six-month-old child in her lap. 'What's the matter with my son, is it bad?' The doctor seemed not to hear a word.

The brother came with the medicine. A red mixture, morphine, that settled the chest and dampened the man's cough. There was grief in this home. It was a grief that had come so very suddenly. There the man lay, pale and still, and his young wife did not sleep. Was it really her dearest friend who lay so helpless and sick, so perilously sick that she must nurse and watch over him?

The next day towards evening he suffered another fierce coughing fit, and again there was blood, though unlike the day before it did not come bubbling and spluttering, but instead seemed coagulated, in lumps and clots. Now there was a pain in his chest, which had not been there the day before. The doctor was sent for, but the patient was to remain still, and with ice in his mouth. Some was duly fetched from the dairy, and now there was someone at his bed day and night. Days passed. He lay in the chamber, his life in the balance. His voice was no longer strong enough to be heard, unless they came very close to him. The cough had settled itself in his lungs, and indeed all that was human in him had ground to a halt. Thus the patient lay for thirteen days, still on his back, without clean sheets, without sitting up. The priest visited, and the man received the Eucharist, and afterwards they sang 'Thy mercy, O Lord, is in the heavens.'

But spring was before them, and life in the sickroom began to turn. The patient took more nourishment, and his voice was restored. Hopes rose, the man's sheets were now changed and he was allowed to turn over in his bed, and how good it felt. The doctor said to the young wife: 'Now let's try to get him on his feet, and in a few days when the weather is fine he can sit out in the sun.' And then, almost as an aside: 'He'll be looking after the hens when summer comes.' The man then understood the nature of his ailment. 'Is it the consumption?' he asked. The doctor explained what measures should be taken and laid out his instructions so as to avoid contagion within the family. Only then did they truly comprehend what had happened. A man or woman smitten in their best age would always succumb. When the man and his wife were alone, the man said: 'Now you must never kiss me again,' and both of them wept.

The man's brother remained there and took up the work that spring. The man would repeat to himself the words of the doctor: 'He'll be looking after the hens when autumn comes. And,' the man added, 'by autumn, when the cold comes with winter at its back, I shall be in the black soil.'

Already in May that year the weather was delightful and summery. And such fortune it was that the man had planted the saplings and hedgerows, for now he could shuffle about and lie sheltered from the wind and sun. His wife took his bedding outside into the garden so that he might lie there in comfort. These were strenuous days for the young wife. The man could see it, he noticed when she dressed in the mornings how his spouse grew skinnier by the day. One day, he lay outside under the trees and as so often before prayed for himself and those he held dear, that he might fully recover, if that is the best for me and my loved ones, but if it is not thy will, then take me home to you, Lord, as your child, and then he prayed for his wife and child, take them in your strong hands, Lord, and my aged mother, comfort and strengthen her too. And at that moment his wife suddenly stood over him, and her tears fell into her husband's face. She wrung her hands and smoothed his hair. I heard your prayer, and was compelled to come to you. Thank you, my dearest friend. And both of them wept.

October 20

Grell wished only to show me something that might comfort me. It *does* comfort me. It hurts me too.

~

What would Vigand think on the matter, if he saw me sitting here? How would he advise me?

I can almost hear his voice. He is in no doubt.

Get this mess cleaned up, and let some air in. You're not *that* interesting.

October 21

Today I have tidied up and aired the rooms. I threw open all the windows, which sent the sea of papers on the floor of Vigand's study into turmoil. I returned the books to their rightful places, tidied the drawers, and closed everything behind me. The downstairs rooms were thus becalmed. But upstairs are his clothes. Should I take this lovely row of soap-scented shirts with me when I move? What about his pressed jackets and waistcoats? His dressing gown and his smoking jacket that is now so threadbare at the elbows. The brown suit, the black suit, the grey suit? The shoes that carried his steady feet? Vigand was a handsome man.

In a sudden fit, I threw out the pajamas, underwear and shaving tackle he had taken with him to the hospital. I carried the bundle down to the incinerator in the garden and set it aflame. It made a smoky fire, continually on the verge of going out. I stood and poked it with a stick, eventually deciding to leave it alone, and went back in – only to return again shortly afterwards. The fire had already died out, and was not even smoldering. Some holes had been burnt in the clothing, that was all. I doused the embers with household spirit. They flared up for a second, then dwindled away again. It was not because of rain, though the air was damp. Its greyness is without bounds. Eventually, I emptied the bottle of spirit into the incinerator and turned the contents about with the stick, and when I tossed a match into it the flames leapt up so suddenly they singed my hair. When I brush it now, little particles of grey-black descend onto the dresser.

Hilda came at about three o'clock with some flat cakes she had baked. She called them *lapper* cakes. She stood on the step and patted them awkwardly as she told me about them. "*Uh, t'l bae s'queet now in t'town,*" she said mournfully. I invited her in for coffee. She was afraid to be a bother, and I almost had to push her into the living room. I was going to put her cakes out on the table, but she would hear nothing of it; they lacked the standard, she said. I insisted. They were drab and mushy, but tasted good. "There's lemon in them," I said, and she mustered a smile. And there we sat, one widow facing another.

Hilda has become so tiny and reaches no higher than to my chest. Her features, formerly sharp, pinched to their raw essence, are now flushed and indistinct. Once, her eyes lustred as if she were forever running a temperature. Now they are dull. She alternates between weeping and laughter, entirely unprompted. "Things will be all right, they shall have to be," she has always said. She lives on the charity of the parish. There was a time when she did jobs for people, she took on all that she could manage, and had the daylights beaten out of her when she got home. When she came here crying over her husband's death, Vigand told her: "You're well rid of him. You've been waiting for years."

And today she came and showed me that she bore no malice.

When Vigand had his practice moved here to the town eight years ago, we used to see quite a lot of Hilda. She came creeping. "*Uh, t'dowtor ee'll av eneugh tae bae giddin on wae,*" she would say, not wishing to be any trouble, and then lift her face to reveal a shining, swollen eye. Whenever she spoke unflatteringly about her husband Karl, she would immediately take it back. "Oh, but Karl can't see it, and why should he, he's a man, and such things lie beyond a man's reason." She was clinging to her dignity, I see that now, but at one point Vigand had had enough. Hilda had come to us with two teeth knocked out of her lower jaw, the blood hung from her chin in filaments. After he had treated her, he came in and asked me to sit with her for a while. "Let her talk," he said. "It'll do her good while I'm gone."

"Where are you going?" I asked.

"Out."

He put his coat on and went. Hilda and I sat in the living room. She was in a state and said nothing, but it was not her injured mouth that was foremost in her mind. She kept glancing towards the door. But Vigand was not gone for very long. After a short time we heard him return to the consulting room, and Hilda's unrest grew. She sat there with her back straight, perspiring. I went and knocked on the door.

"I think Hilda's waiting," I said.

"Oh, yes," he said, looking up from some papers as if he had forgotten all about us. "Tell her she can go home now. It won't happen again."

"I think you should tell her yourself."

"No, you tell her."

"I imagine she'd like to thank you."

He sighed. He never understood people's gratitude. It was a burden to him that people should "lean" on him in such a way, he said. Grudgingly, he went in to speak to her while I waited in the consulting room.

Later it was rumored in the town and the outlying district that the doctor had gone to Karl Madsen and told him that if he ever touched Hilda again, he, Vigand, would personally make sure he could never raise a hand again.

I loved him for that.

Widows are a community. I have been aware of it ever since I was a child. It can be seen in the way they seek each other's company, in the pews for instance, where often they will sit in pairs. They do not speak much, for they have no need, and after the service they go their separate ways. In my childhood home, the widows sat together at meals and at work in the workroom.

It is a matter of having lived with one person for most of one's adult life, and to have lost that person. To have been set free. Freedom is not always a good thing. There is a freedom in which one is unseen. Such is the life of the widow. When the days of mourning are gone, and grief has become tiresome to one's surroundings, one ceases to be an interesting person and must accept the fact. Widows possess an experience that is not understood by others. They must live with becoming grey in the eyes of the world, and have lost their right of protest, for they are outside the common community.

As outcasts they stick together. But that is not the only

reason. There is a warmth there, and understanding. They are acquainted with things.

We have our dead. Our hope is that we too will be someone's.

We sat in the bay window and had our coffee.

I have no idea how long Karl Madsen kept his hands from Hilda. Vigand's threats worked long enough for us to believe the matter to be concluded, and Vigand perhaps especially. For that reason he had no patience with her grief when it started again, by then he had lost interest and found it tactless of her to come knocking. He had repaired her once already. Why did she have to come apart again? And yet he sent her in to me, and we sat together in the living room. I was furious that Hilda became quite frightened. This will not do! I said. It must cease! You can come and live here, Hilda. You can help us out with the housework.

Oh, but I couldn't, she sniveled, and buried her beaten face in her hands.

And perhaps she was right. What if Karl Madsen had come and caused trouble? Who would then have been put into the street? Not heavy-handedly, perhaps. But put into the street, nonetheless. She would have been worse off than before. And what would Vigand have said anyway, to see her trembling figure in his scullery when he came down in the mornings? To see her fussing about with winter curtains and step ladders in the living room? Or to follow, through the window of the consulting room, her exertions with a carpet beater at the rack in the back garden? He would have held me responsible for her entire existence.

What would I have said?

"How long is it now since your husband died?" I asked.

"Three years this April," she replied.

Vigand was a self-sufficient man. No, an industrious man. He became annoyed if ever he was delayed or hindered in his business. He asked for no devotion. No attention, no coddling. Only one thing did he demand: that one should always have something to do. Fussing about, which is what most of us spend our lives doing, was something for which he had no time. Nor did he ever relax. Nowadays one talks of leisure, and relaxing with one's interests. Vigand had no interests, and could not have cared less about relaxing. The closest he ever came to such things was probably the book he wrote when he was still a young man, about tuberculosis, uncleanliness, and the curse of the co-operative movement, which as he saw it consisted of the cut-price sale of albumens and fat in return for concentrated animal feed, artificial fertilizer and field seed, and which had reached the point at which people themselves were suffering for the sake of their livestock and turnover. *The dairies march onwards*, he wrote, *while nutrition declines in the humble abodes, and thus the way is paved for tuberculosis.*

Vigand always had something to do. But occasionally his mind clouded and he would descend into despair. I had no idea what path would take him there. If there were danger signals, he kept them well concealed. But now and then, when I came in with the coffee tray, he would be sitting at his desk and lift his head to look at me with darkness in his eyes and say: "I'm done for!"

And I would say: "Don't you think it's about time you visited Fru Andersen?"

And he would reply: "Yes!"

She lived out in Thyregod Field. Evald Trang Kristenen had written about her. He called her the Field Wife in his book. Her real name was Terkelline Andersen, and she died some nine or ten years ago.

I cannot imagine that Vigand ever visited her in his capacity of physician, and I have no idea how they got to know each other. Fru Andersen was Vigand's chum, and he would go to see her when he needed a good guffaw. Vigand never spoke of laughing in that respect, but always of a good guffaw. She cleanses the soul as good as a bath, he would say of her too.

Few were admitted through her door. Mostly one would see her on market days in Give, where she would cause a stir among the stalls with her pithy talk and shrewd manner. The men would invite her to the public bar of the hotel to see if they could get her drunk, but she would always stop before things got out of hand. She looked out for herself. Zigzagged her way through life. She had a son out of wedlock, Jens Kristian, who had come into the world with a mat of hair all over his body, due to lack of nourishment inside his mother's womb. Today he is a hefty redhead, as stooping as an old man. After his mother died he began to venture out on his own. Now and then one sees him in town, where he goes from door to door selling pins and pencils and the like. But for many years he was seen neither on the roads nor in town. He lay at home in his mother's house on a sagging sofa with an old coat to cover him. On the wall next to him was a shelf for his food. Vigand said Jens Kristian had told him it was bad enough that the mice had the gall to chew on his bread, but worse that they pissed on it too. It was a comment that had Vigand in stitches if he happened to think about it.

Was he laughing at him or with him, I wonder? To him there was no difference. It amounted to the same. Fru Andersen was a tonic for his melancholy, and for that he respected her. He once said that he admired her. As I sit here now, thinking about everything and nothing, I recall that he actually went to her funeral. It was a day in May. The church was packed. The young chestnuts on the bank were in leaf. Vigand went to a funeral.

At some point, a man came into Fru Andersen's life. His name was Nygaard and apparently he had been in the dragoons. One of his arms was missing after he fell from a cart onto a plough blade and had to have it amputated. He earned a meager income as a rag-and-bone man. The bed of his cart was always covered with a tarpaulin so no one could see what was in it. He slept here and there in barns, where he could find fodder for his horse. One might reasonably say of Nygaard that he had sunk to the bottom. He came to her a stray and remained there. They even got married.

He kept a den out by an old gravel pit, with spruce and old sacking for a bed. He lived there for periods of time to escape Fru Andersen's beatings. That too had Vigand in stitches. Nygaard showed him the place, and Vigand found it to be a splendid solution.

Shortly before she died I took the folklore collector Evald Tang Kristensen out to Thyregod Field to visit Fru Andersen, whom he had heard to be a treasure trove of folk tales and ballads. He had approached me, because we had made each other's acquaintance during my time at the free school when he had once encouraged some of the children to tell him stories. So I took him out there one frosty day when the air was as crisp and clear as it is only seldom in these parts, where the tendency is more to dampness and wind. Heather, grass, and sand were mantled with white. A low sun hung over the flat land. Evald Tang Kristensen bustled as he went, and walked rather briskly for such a heavy man. I almost had to trot to keep up. In the distance a house appeared. 'That must be the place,' he said. I begged to differ. Even from afar it seemed clear that the house was abandoned and that no one had lived there for a long time. One end of the roof had fallen in. The faded beams jutted into the dark void, and as we came closer we saw holes that gaped in the walls. An entire section, the size of a gateway, was missing in the middle, and some sheeting had been hung up to stop the gap. There was a chimney, but no smoke. A ladder stood leaned against the roof, and the yard was littered with junk. We went inside and found Fru Andersen lying in her bed. She stayed there when it was cold, she said, for there was no stove in the house, and what good would a fire do anyway with the house open to the weather? But she was pleased to see us and eager to talk. There were no chairs to sit on. Evald Tang Kristensen produced his notebook and kneeled down on an old box so that he could reach the table to write, and so as not to disturb them I went outside and heard on my way the strangest screeching song, a diminishing and then abruptly rising monotone that accompanied me over the flat, frost-covered ground. Like a great, lifeless bird suddenly flapping into the sky. Without reason.

November 1

I attended church today and listened to Grell talk on the Beatitudes.

I found a seat behind the tiled stove, tucked away where I could not be seen. It was a raw and bitter day, and although the sexton lit the fire last evening, carpets of icy damp air gusted through the interior. People coughed. We are soon at that season. There was a time when all rooms were filled with coughing throughout the year. That is no longer the case. Much has happened since I came to the town, when dust and spittoons together were still a threat to us all. I was not a frequent churchgoer in those years. I will not say I am a stranger to the church, for I am familiar with it and with what goes on there, as one might be familiar with an aging aunt whom one has not visited in a very long time, and when eventually one does, one recognizes straight away the smells of her kitchen and the way in which the old armchair so snugly accommodates the frame as soon as one obliges the invitation to take a seat: everything is exactly as it was when one was a child.

And one acknowledges, too, a twinge of guilt that may indicate that some time will pass before one visits again.

Pastor Grell is no fire-and-brimstone preacher. He reads rather beautifully. His sermon touched on how, as we remember our dead, they remind us silently of the deathly circumstance of our human life. We mourn our dead and we mourn the world, we mourn others, and we mourn ourselves and the things we have and have not done, he said, and cited Kierkegaard, who says that it is the business of the mourner to mourn. Indeed, it is the mourner's obligation; a responsibility with which he is entrusted. Salvation, he said, gives us solace, in that it does not take from us our grief, unlike happiness, which glints and glitters and is disinterested in everything but itself. I sat behind the rumbling stove and embraced his words.

After the service, I remained seated and did not rise until the last of the congregation had gone. But when I stepped out into the entryway, Peter Carlsen was talking to Grell and his wife. Carl was there too, and Dagmar and Inge, who had just returned from folk high school. The two girls are inseparable. Inge was born deaf and is for that reason also dumb, but three years ago she became blind. For a long time after that her only connection to the world was her sister's hand.

But now, Dagmar told me, both had learned braille. How on earth did they manage that? Their teachers at the school were exceptionally skilled, Dagmar said. But how could Inge learn what those dots might mean? An understanding must have developed along the way, baffling to an outsider, in the same way as no one else has ever been able to grasp the meaning of the squeezes they have given each other's hands since they were small children. Perhaps they have been able to understand each other ever since they lay together in their mother's womb. It is as mysterious as the great flocks of birds that suddenly turn as one in the sky. Often I have stood and watched the starlings as they angle this way and that. I have never fathomed it. They are two beautiful young girls. Fair-haired and blue-eyed, each with a long plait that falls between their shoulders.

Peter Carlsen took my hand.

"Good afternoon, Fru Bagge," he said.

"Good afternoon, Peter Carlsen," I said.

Nothing more was spoken, since Pastor Grell interrupted us to mention the memorial service, which he hoped had been in Vigand's spirit. He was different now than the priest in the pulpit, as if he were intent on becoming this younger, more affable man.

I can still feel that handshake. His hand was warm.

It had gone dark when we came out. I did not proceed to the gate, but cut through the churchyard and the little opening in the bank to the west. Halfway home on the empty footpath, someone had placed a ghostly head in the warm slurry of Vester's muck heap. A hollowed-out turnip with eyes, nose and mouth, a candle stump inside. A row of grinning teeth. Ha ha ha. The light flickered at me. Ha ha ha! I smiled back obligingly and went home to myself where I put some peat on the fire.

I lit the lamp.

HALLOW-EVE

The heath is desolate, though not deserted. Darkness will soon descend. It is three o'clock and the road stretches out in front of the carriage, madly winding, despite the fact that there are neither boundaries nor dwellings nor private land to take into consideration. Like a stream that meanders with age, the road meanders too. Now and then byways open out like a fan. There are deltas and tributaries, and occasionally, quite without warning or any flourish of vegetation, a stream with trickling black heathwater escaped from the sour earth. The carriage jolts and creaks. It plunges into holes and is pulled free again, continually on the verge of grinding to a halt. Brorson is on a visitation and his wife has accompanied him. They have left Thyregod Rectory and are on their way to Øster Nykirke. The light dwindles. They did not leave until rather late. It is Hallow-Eve, 1760.

"Is it wrong of me to write such a thing in my report?" he asks.

"On the contrary, it is quite appropriate," she replies.

What is there to say of his report? It is briefer than usual.

He holds his hand over the priest and parish. But of the parish clerk's house he will write: "Never have I seen one in such miserable repair."

He places a hand on her thigh and closes his eyes. She knows his stomach is paining him, and being tossed about the carriage in such a way can only make it worse. She strokes his aged, thankful hand. It is big and warm and open.

She looks out the window and is astonished to see an animal running alongside. At first she thinks it to be a wolf. But it is powerful and muscular, not lean and mangy like the wolves of the heath. It is black as coal.

A dog.

She strokes her husband's hand. This is lawless country, and the night too is itself without law. Now the living and the dead go amongst each other. If the carriage were to stop and they step out into the darkness, they would sense that the night has become alive.

The dog runs with the carriage. It does not lag behind, nor increase its speed. After the horse has hauled them out of a rut, she thinks it to be gone. And yet it is there again.

Then, suddenly, it is there no more.

"Look," she says. "It's snowing."

He opens his eyes and sees it to be true. Such an early

time for snow. A few solitary flakes to begin with, presently a flurry. He presses his cheek to the pane and peers upwards. He whispers to himself. She finds a piece of paper and slips it under his hand.

~

The rectory at Thyregod is a quadrangle of farm buildings around an inner yard. Besides the priest and his wife it houses a farm boy and a servant girl of twelve years old, and the priestly couple's youngest son, a weakling who lies in the alcove spitting blood. Moreover, there is the sister of the priest's wife, who sits glumly on a commode from which she will not rise. There should also be a laborer on the farm. But it is the *skiftedag*, the day on which help may lawfully change employment, and the laborer went his way two days ago. His replacement, who was supposed to have come this morning, has yet to arrive. Often, new help exploit the day to attend to private matters and will first appear two or three days late. There is nothing to be done about it. People manage without.

The boy and the girl huddle together at the stove. All day the girl has been absorbed in a great flock of birds she noticed had come to rest on the flat piece of land beyond the bank of the kitchen garden when they got up this morning, and which has yet to move from it. The birds are the size of jays, brown and mottled, with light-colored spots. All day long the air has been full of their *kra-kra-kra*, but their cry is higher-pitched than the crow's. The boy says they have come from Russia and are meant to be on their way to the Black Sea, and that they have taken a wrong turn. There is no food for them here, he says. They will die if they stay, but perhaps they are too weak now to fly on.

How does he know such things? He has said there once were great forests here, and that if one digs in the boglands one may find thick trunks of the oak that stood here thousands of years ago. He showed her a barrel plug he had carved from such a piece of wood. It is almost black, and hard as stone. He keeps it in his pocket. He says that just as the land here was once covered by forest, so it may be again at some future time. The heath as they know it will not remain for always.

"Do you think the birds are cold?" she asks.

"Yes," says the boy. "But perhaps they are really expired souls, on their way from their graves to the kingdom of the dead. We should set an extra place at the table before we go to bed tonight," he says. "But we can also leave some food out on the floor, it's just as good."

~

That evening there is a hammering at the rectory gate.

The priest is at his desk, weary after the bishop's visitation. He puts his pen down on the paper, on which he has written: *God and the parishioners alike know only too well that no one here has been of means as far back as any can recall. And it is hardly remarkable, in this smallest and humblest living of the county, this most meager and impoverished of parishes . . .*

The farm is shut up for the night.

The hammering resumes. The priest rises. He is an old man, pale with fatigue. Passing through the kitchen he encounters his wife.

"What is it?" she asks.

"Someone's knocking."

"We can't take anyone in," she says.

"Listen," he says.

They listen.

"You mustn't answer," she says.

"I shall tell them to go on to the inn at Hjortsballe."

"No," she says.

But he goes out. She scurries after him and shouts from the doorstep: "Then send them to Sønder Farm at Dørken. Sometimes they take folk in there, and it's not as far."

She sees his lamp cross the yard through the whipping snow. He works the bolt aside and pulls at the heavy wooden gate. Barely a crack appears before a beast thrusts its way through into the yard. The priest staggers backwards, startled.

It is a dog.

The priest's attention is diverted. After the dog comes a man, riding on a bull. They fill the gateway, and the priest is pressed back against the wall.

"Tell them to go to Sønder Farm at Dørken," the priest's wife shrieks from the doorway of the house. But it is too late. The man, the bull, and the dog are already in.

The bull is put in the stable. The dog remains untethered and runs around the yard. The man and the priest enter the house. The priest's wife stands in the entrance hall and receives them warily.

The guest knocks the snow from his hat, turns and addresses her. Bewildered, she says to her husband:

"I can't understand him."

"He's from the Rhineland," her husband replies. "Fetch us some food."

"Food?"

The priest avoids her gaze.

"Yes, food."

The pantry is full of food after the bishop's visitation, though to be kept, not eaten now. She instructs the girl to warm some milk and find a plate of cold porridge.

"Do you want me to take it in?" the girl asks.

"No," says the priest's wife. "I'll take it in myself."

With trembling hands she carries the milk and the porridge to the table. In the light inside, the man sits smoking a pipe whose bowl is hardly bigger than an acorn. He is thin and bears a festering wound on his forehead.

"Who is he?" she asks.

"A discharged soldier," says the priest.

"I thought as much."

"He was in a shipwreck. When he got home, his sweetheart had made off with someone else. His knee is bad too."

"He told you this?"

"His mind ails nothing," says the priest.

"He's a *night-man*, a gypsy," says the wife.

"He says his name is Vater," says the priest.

At the sound of his name the man lifts his head.

"Tell him to put out his pipe," she says.

"There's no need."

"Tell him to put it out now."

She goes to sit with her son. An unhuman warmth issues from his body. The vapors of his sweat these past few weeks have paled the woodwork of his bed. She takes a cloth and wipes his face. His hand brushes hers. He is awake and knows her. She bends over him and sees his blood spat on the wall. She wipes his face, and wipes it again.

"It's snowing," she says. "It'll be a hard winter."

He mumbles something. His breath too is burning hot, his exhausted body respires fiercely.

A thought comes to her.

"I'll be back in a minute." She gets to her feet and tells the boy and the girl to fill a bucket with snow and bring it to her. They put on their overcoats and go out into the yard, are gone for some time. They return with snow in their hair, their shoulders and backs speckled with it, cheeks ruddy. They put the bucket down at her feet.

"I heard you singing," she says.

"But we weren't," they say.

"But indeed you were," she insists.

"No," they say.

So strange everything is this night.

"They've brought you snow," she says to her son. "Give me your hand." She places some snow in his hand. It melts immediately and runs into the bedding, and he smiles a barely conscious, delirious and grateful smile that passes fleetingly over his face and does not return.

She goes back to fetch the empty bowl and is startled to a halt in the doorway. A second man has come. He is not very tall, but fuller in figure than the first, with dark and shiny hair. He sits and smokes a pipe the same as the one she saw before. Neither of the two men seems to notice her. There is a bottle on the table.

"Bering," she says with a groan. The second man rises to his feet and bows, but she pays him no heed.

"What is this, Bering?"

"Everything's fine," her husband says. "They're on their way to Randbøl. They need a place for the night."

"How did he get in?"

"We let him in."

We most certainly did not, she says to herself.

"And what's that bottle doing there? Tell them to put out their pipes. Make them understand. The house could burn down, and then where would we be?" She steps forward with her hand outstretched, stamps her foot and gestures to be given the pipes. Her husband bows his head.

He is the authority.

Authority resides here, this house is the pivot of the law in the two far-flung parishes of Thyregod and Vester. And yet they do not feel safe. No one is here to help them, and no one can now come in.

"We'll be murdered in our beds," she says out loud. The men surrender their pipes. "The bottle as well." She gestures. The second man hands her the bottle. The grin on his face nearly makes her nauseous.

The boy and the girl sit huddled together at the stove when she returns to the kitchen. They have contrived to fall asleep and yet keep each other upright. The girl clutches a dark wooden barrel plug in her hand. She wakes them up. "Go to bed," she says. "You need to sleep."

When they have left her and she is alone, she takes the silver goblets and the spoons from the shelf and wraps them up in layers of cloth. Quietly she opens the door. In the stable she finds a spade. She opens the gate, and then she is outside. The dog was not there. Perhaps they have tied it somewhere. It is still snowing. She follows the wall of the stable. The heath comes right up to the buildings, only the kitchen garden, where the curly kale pokes from the earth and a pair of gooseberry bushes likewise break the flatness, is amenable to digging. She lays the silverware on the ground and thrusts the spade into the soil. The frost is as yet only at the surface, and though she is old there is still a strength in her body.

When she has dug the hole and placed the items in the ground and covered them up, she realizes the air is full of sounds. At first she thinks it to be the rush of her blood, but indeed it is song, passing over into a whisper in which mingle the sounds of rattling bridles and horses whinnying, as though a whole procession were riding through the night. She lifts her head; the sky is black. There is nothing to see but the snow. The snow, spilling from the sky.

When she returns inside, the house has retired. Her husband has gone to bed. The two men lie in the baking oven. But she remains up. She sits with her son. The snow has melted in the bucket. She wrings a cloth in its water and washes his hands and face. No candle or lamp has she lit. His spirit seems to have dwindled, it feels like she is sitting with the very dimness of his being now, as she strokes his hair and cheeks and brow. Now and then she gets to her feet and goes out onto the step and listens. The night is still now. The procession has ridden on. It has passed. In the baking oven the men are calm. Each time she looks, they are lying in the same position as the last time.

As the hours progress she goes between her son, the sleeping guests, and the step.

And then, when morning comes and she looks into the baking oven, she looks directly into a pair of open eyes. Vater is sitting upright.

In a moment his feet are on the floor, he calls to his companion over his shoulder. His hands fumble with his clothing, his trousers. She tries to dart away, but he grabs her and holds her back. He bends down and deposits a handful of soil-dusted tubers on the floor. "*Ertaapeln*," he says. He mimes digging with a spade. He places a tuber in the hole he has dug in the air and covers it up. He looks at her shrewdly. "*Gut*," he says.

There are thirteen in all. She turns on her heels.

"Bering," she shouts. "They're leaving. Help them with the bull."

As soon as they are gone, she takes one of the tubers and tosses it on the muck heap. The rest she leaves on the floor. Shortly, the boy and girl come in.

"They're potatoes," says the boy. "They grow in sandy earth. People think them poisonous." He fetches a sock and puts the potatoes inside, and buries them in the straw of his bed. "In a hundred years," he says, "the heath will be gone."

"I don't believe it," says the girl.

"In time we shall be fat and rich and sated. In time there will be fields here. By then, all people will be able to read."

"I don't believe it," the girl says again.

"Wait and see," says the boy.

November 4

A free-school teacher must be able to tell a story, for storytelling is the heart of any teaching. Whenever I told the children about the potato-Germans who came up here and became a part of the great movement that together with rationalism formed the very beginnings of the society we know today, I told them about Vater who came riding on a bull and in thanks for the hospitality he received at the rectory gave the pastor's wife thirteen potatoes. Sometimes I made him an imposing, self-assured man, on other occasions he was a poor wretch who could be mistaken with any one among the hordes of beggars who vagabonded through Europe at that time. The children liked the thought that Brorson found his inspiration for *Behold a Host, Arrayed in White* in Thyregod, and that it was from Thyregod that the potato spread throughout the land, and they would ask what became of the clever boy. "Perhaps he is the great-great-grandfather of one of you," I would suggest in reply. On other occasions, I told them he went to Copenhagen and became a renowned biologist. It would set them thinking. Could someone renowned come from Thyregod? Yes, I would say, think of Grundtvig. But the children did not find Grundtvig to be a good example, since he lived here only a few short years. Was it possible to go to Copenhagen? Everything is possible, I said. Think of Anders Blikker's father, who visited America almost thirty years ago. We often ventured out on the wings of our imaginations, instead of concentrating on facts and realities as we were supposed to.

Sometimes they told me stories of their own. One of them, which I recall to this day since it puzzled me so, went like this: When Brande Church was being built there was a troll who lived in Thyregod, and the troll became so angry he picked up a mighty rock and hurled it at the tower. But the rock missed and landed in the beck out at Krusborg. There were five marks on the rock.

It left me perplexed. "What do the five marks mean?" I asked.

"They don't mean anything."

"Then why do you tell the story?"

"Because there were five marks on it."

"How do you know?"

"There just were."

"But have you seen the rock?"

They fell silent. Then one of them said yes, and cast me a furtive glance. Others had seen it too, it quickly turned out.

That aided my understanding somewhat. And yet the story left me strangely unsettled. The children, however, were most satisfied, though may possibly have felt unsettled themselves for having lied.

Today I went to speak to Peder Møllergaard, manager of the savings bank and chairman of the parish council. Until a few years ago, the savings bank had its address in his private home at Lunds Farm, but now they have an office at the temperance hotel and are open every Thursday in the late afternoon.

"Good afternoon, Fru Bagge," he said.

"Good afternoon, Peder Møllergaard," I replied.

"And so the time has come for us to discuss matters," he said.

"Yes," I said.

"Do have a seat, Fru Bagge."

Even now, in his early eighties, he is one of the tallest men in the parish, and moreover solidly built. So big and callused are his hands, and covered in senile warts, that when shaking his hand in greeting one feels oneself to be but the wispiest breath of a very young girl. I have seen him draw barbed wire as one would draw a rope.

In the summer of 1864, still referred to as the Dry Summer, need was so great here in the district that not even the heather could provide fodder enough for the winter. When Peder Møllergaard one evening stood and looked out over the rough and arid land, the very sight of it brought tears to his eyes, and because he wept so, he realized that something had to be done. Thus, the savings bank was founded. There were twelve depositors in all, each deposit between three and five rigsdalers in sum.

I have always been moved by the thought of the man who stood and wept at the side of his house, not for want of strength, but out of love for the land from which he came, and when at school I told the children about the savings bank and how much it has meant for our town in allowing those of humble means the opportunity to borrow and invest, that is what I told them.

Peder Møllergaard opened a drawer and took out a

document. He put on his spectacles and read through what was written, his head moving slowly from side to side as his eyes passed over the lines, peering over the rim of the spectacles.

"This letter in my hand, Fru Bagge," he said, "is from your husband."

"Yes," I said.

"He was aware of his plight. And he has taken care of matters. I would say that he has taken very good care indeed, Fru Bagge." And then he mentioned a sum. The result, he said, of a sale of bonds during the summer, deposited in an account in my name.

I was so taken aback, I spluttered: "I had no idea Vigand *had* any bonds."

"I imagine he wished for you not to bother your mind with the matter, Fru Bagge," Peder Møllergaard replied, and folded the letter. I did not inquire about anything else. But now I cannot help but wonder where those bonds came from. I never knew his parents, and Vigand was uninformative as to his background, but I suppose there was an inheritance, for if there is one thing I do know, it is that the money cannot have come from his practice, since his patients were seldom able to pay for his consultations, and more frequently were released from the debt. They said in the town that Dr. Bagge would positively bark at those who stood before him and clutched their coins, and would tell them to keep such a pittance, did they honestly believe it made any difference to him? I must confess that I always thought it to be chivalry, but perhaps it was actually the pure and unembellished truth.

I said goodbye to Peder Møllergaard and left.

I am shaken.

He told me that as chairman of the parish council he would naturally be interested to learn of any change in my circumstances. He was thinking of my impending move. "It is indeed satisfying to know, Fru Bagge," he said, "that you can have things any way you want."

I could move back to Fyn, if that is what I want.

I feel like a person standing in a landscape so empty and open that it matters not a bit in which direction I choose to go. There would be no difference: north, south, east, or west, it would be the same wherever I went.

$\sim$

I have lit the lamp. I have written to Line and told her that I sent her dresser with the carrier today. And I have written to Dr. Eriksen and told him that I should like to buy back the car.

November 10

It is slaughtering time. From the butcher Schnedler's farm come the most terrifying squeals.

I caught the train to Give at midday and walked up to the hospital, where Dr. Eriksen had brought the car out. He was embarrassed by the situation and we dealt hurriedly with the business. He asked how I was thinking of getting it home, and I told him I would drive. He got to his feet to accompany me outside, but I declined and said there was nothing to worry about, which seemed to relieve him somewhat. I saw nothing of Nurse Svendsen.

I have sat beside Vigand enough times to know how one starts a motor car and which pedal is the brake, which the clutch and the accelerator. First, I drove out in the direction of Riis, then eventually turned back to Give and parked in the street outside the police station.

"I've come to obtain a driver's licence," I said to Jonassen, who also happens to be the vehicle inspector, and took him over to the bay window, where I pointed out.

"How did that vehicle arrive here?" he wanted to know.

"I drove it," I told him.

The information was sufficient for him to return to his desk and issue the document to me. I paid the four kroner it cost and received a stamp. I am now the holder of a driver's licence.

Sometimes things are so easy, at other times so hard as to defy comprehension.

Speaking of things being easy: I received my education from the Ringe School of Education, where for two years I was a student of Rasmus Laursen. There were six of us in my year, and Dagny Nielsen and I were the only girls. She died at an early age, many years ago now. I made good friends at Ringe. Dagny, of course, and also two young men, whose names were Erland and Ervin. We lodged in different parts of the town and would meet up in the evenings after lessons. Once, when Erland and Ervin were sitting in my room, which I had rented from a seamstress, Erland began to laugh so much he tipped backwards on his chair against a wallpapered partition and disappeared through a hole into the seamstress's chamber. He talked loudly, sang loudly, laughed loudly, and was the most helpful person I have ever known. If ever I told him to quiet down, he would lower his blushing face to mine and dampen his voice. But he would always want to discuss a matter, and would go on until it no longer made sense and everyone had wearied of it.

Ervin was different entirely. It was as if he gave out a light, and that light surrounded him; he was a good listener, and quite refined. He was happy in himself, and always remembered the people he had encountered, no matter the circumstance. He made them feel known.

One time when we were out on teaching practice, Ervin and I went over to botanize in a corner of the meadow that ran up to the school. The idea was to make a survey of what we found and then send the children out in the next lesson to gather plants for a herbarium. We would then be able to shine with our knowledge. We had each taken a handbook of flowers with us in our pockets, and yet we still found specimens we were unable to look up. "Can't we just pull them up?" I suggested, and as he stood and gaped at me his face widened into a laugh, and at that moment it felt like something sank inside my chest.

In the winter we skated on the pond. One night, Ervin and I went there on our own. We skated under the moon. It was a half-moon, its light was so bright it cast shadows. There were reeds at the bank. The sounds that can come from a frozen pond on such a night: the skates, and the humming and singing beneath the ice when pockets of gas are set in motion and shoot from one end to another. We skated alongside each other with hands crossed, when suddenly the ice cracked with a sharp report, we plunged and found ourselves in water to the waist. He lifted me up and put me down on the edge of the ice, and afterwards I managed to haul him up too. We ran home as fast as we could, wild with laughter.

So much joy between us. It felt like the world would forever be new. How marvelous it would be to hear that laughter again. I see the meadow in my mind, or rather the light above the meadow. In my recollection it is almost white. Oddly, Ervin's hair is almost white too, the same color as the bleached grass, the pale light.

At the School of Education we were instructed in botany, the history of the Nordic region, geography, Danish, arithmetic, storytelling, the Bible, world history, pedagogy, reading, music, and drawing, as well as in summer half an hour of physical education each day. But above all we learned what would be expected of us when our training was complete and we were to engage with a circle of parents as well as children. It was impressed upon us that while the ideal of the free school was one thing, with its emphasis on culture and freedom and its eschewal of exams, it was quite another to be cast into its everyday practice. Rasmus Laursen, who took us in pedagogy, told us this: "You cannot change the world, and if you think it must adapt to you, then you are very much mistaken."

But I, who had attended Ryslinge, dreamed of the Folk High School, and as our graduation approached I wrote to Ryslinge's principal, Didriksen, whom I knew from my time there, and asked if he might have need of me to teach needlework, Danish history, and physical education for girls, and when I told Ervin what I had done he said right away: "Then I'll do the same." Again, that sinking feeling inside my chest, which I honestly recall to be a sudden sense of plummeting, as when a house abruptly settles, and I was so startled by it that I began to laugh. And he laughed too.

November 12

It has caused a stir that I have become a motorist. People come and visit. They do not appear to be dissatisfied by it. "It was sad the doctor and the car went at the same time," said Hilda and laughed for a moment before halting abruptly in dismay and bursting into tears, and today when I was in town to buy coffee, the grocer Rosenstand reminded me that I had been the first lady of the town to ride a bicycle. Yet the butcher Schnedler says: "I hope you're not intending to drive off for good?"

For the time being, I content myself with little journeys in order to get used to the vehicle. Yesterday I was at Sejrup and Haarsbjerg Plantation. The people of the district find the straight rows of trees to be handsome. They are unfamiliar with deciduous woods and would most likely not even think them preferable, for they prefer nothing that cannot thrive in these parts. But not so long ago, even pine forest was an impossible thought. Twenty or thirty years ago there was nothing here but heather-clad hills and a very few stunted oaks, never taller than a child, and now this magnificent forest of white spruce and mountain pine. I climbed out of the car. It felt like there was an intake of breath between the trees, a stillness of something momentarily held back, as if the trees were breathing. After a short time, the animals that had crept into concealment began to emerge. Mice and squirrels. And goldcrests chirped among the branches.

When the heathland here was planted up, I think I allowed the children off school for a time so they could help with the work. At any rate, there hangs a picture in the parish book collection of perhaps a dozen free-school pupils in aprons, with buckets containing saplings of white spruce, taken one early morning before they began their job. I think they earned money from it. The boys also earned money driving lambs from the sheds of the inn, where buyers came, to Kollemorten, and those who were lucky could earn money putting skittles back up in the inn's skittle alley, though this was mostly the preserve of Oscar and Janus, the proprietor's own boys.

Emptying out my drawers after Vigand's death, I found an old school photograph. It was taken outside my accommodation, at the south side of the building. It must have been a day in spring. There are no trees in the yard, so there is no way of telling what time of year it was taken, apart perhaps from the mud on the children's wooden shoes, and the sunlight, which is sharp. I have looked at that picture quite a bit: their faces, their shoes, their clothes, but most of all their faces. I have looked especially at the faces of the smallest ones. There is something either scowling or faint-hearted about many of them, even verging on the simple-minded. Perhaps it is due to their being so unaccustomed to having their photographs taken. I am no better myself, and look nothing like I would wish.

A few of them, and Oscar and Janus in particular come to mind, were mischief-makers.

All were children used to hard work. One summer, Anders Blikker's two boys were sent off with copperware on two long poles across their shoulders and told not to come home until the lot was sold. They walked to Nørre Snede, continued north and were gone more than a fortnight. Where did they sleep? In barns here and there. What did they see, and who did they talk to? I have no idea. They were no more than eight or nine years old. Without doubt they encountered both goodness and malice. One can only hope that goodness was the greater.

As one must hope in general.

From the age of ten, the boys could drive a pair of horses

in front of a harrow, and when they were thirteen they could steer a plough and swing a flail and do all the work of a laborer. And before that they would water and move the cattle. They removed the rocks from the fields. They cut peat in the springtime. The girls looked after children and hens and did housework. They took up potatoes in the autumn and planted them in the spring with an apron full of dung tied about their waists so they could place a dollop on top of each potato. They told of headstrong cows they eventually had to thump with the tethering stake to make them behave. But they told too of larks' nests and play. Each child could have as many as twenty nests they watched until the young had flown. They told of how they swam and fished in the ponds of the meadow, and of the joys of warming their bare feet by stepping in a fresh cowpat when they went out in the early morning to move the cattle and the grass was white with frost. Or their delight to feel the mire slowly seep through a hole in a wooden shoe. They kept lambs and kids, and for a whole year Jens Thiis Hansen took a tame jackdaw with him to school. It sat on his shoulder in lessons and seemed so wise and intelligent, and all of us missed it without exception when it died after having gorged itself on grain from an open sack in the grocer's loft.

They leapt in the straw of the stack-barns and clambered from beam to beam, holding on to the laths of the roof. It was how Jens Thiis met his death.

When they came to school they would be smelling of straw and animals. It was the way the children smelled. Most of all, they smelled of the wind.

I left the car and followed a path into the forest, little more than a deep rut between the trees. After some twenty minutes I came to an overgrown peat bank and on the other side a stone-lined well with a rotten lid strewn with twigs and fallen branches. Sweet cicely was growing there, and gooseberry bushes covered in lichen. It was what remained of the garden of an abandoned heathland holding. Of the house neither foundation nor walls remained, though it could hardly have been more than thirty years since the place was inhabited. But there was a doorstep, on which I sat down.

In such a place in spring one may find daffodils, in summer bleeding hearts and columbines. It is always curious to see such blooms in the inky depths of the forest.

I told Hilda about the place when I came home. She knew it well. "It's name is Knokkelborg," she told me. It turned out the holding had belonged to her mother's sister and that when she was little Hilda had lived there for months on end while her mother died of tuberculosis. "The gooseberries," she said, "they were the best I've ever tasted." I asked if she would care for a drive down the road. She thought not.

Today, however, she changed her mind. We drove up to the station and turned around. She did not wish to be seen in the high street. But at the station we met Carl Carlsen, who was there to photograph the train. He asked if he might take our picture.

And so we were photographed. When it was done, I asked him if he thought Dagmar and Inge might like to go for a drive with me one day.

"Yes," he replied. "One day I think they might."

"What about yourself?" I asked. "Would you like to?"

"No, I don't think I'd like to," he replied.

After some days of increasingly longer drives into the district in Hilda's company, Vigand's voice one evening last week would suddenly not be ignored. "How splendidly charitable of us," he said. "A pity it should smack so much of smugness."

The way he put it struck me as odd, for Vigand did not used to speak in such a stilted manner. What would he have said? "I see you've made friends with Hilda. What's the idea, parading her about like that?"

I was angry. "Mind your own business," I burst out, and brought my plate down hard on the table. "We're having a very nice time together."

And then I was embarrassed at myself and began to cry. He stayed with me all evening. I could not get rid of him. I packed a suitcase, as I now confess to having contemplated on many an occasion while he was alive, and the next day I drove to Fredericia, from where I took the ferry to Strib. I stayed on Fyn for three days, and have only just returned home. The house is so cold that even now after having lit the stoves there is little else to do but go to bed, though the time is hardly past eight o'clock.

November 21

When I applied for the job at Ryslinge I applied for other positions too. It was not easy to find employment in those years, and I was twenty-six years old. I had no desire to go home to my parents, though I would certainly have been a great help to them, nor did I wish to go back to my sister Agnete, for while Heaven knows she could have used me about the house, to lend a hand with the little ones and the milking and the hens and the laundry and the kitchen garden, and though I have never shied away from hard work, I was nevertheless aware that if ever I was to do good for others besides my nearest family, that time was then.

The vacant positions were few. I applied for what there was. Hvalsømagle near Roskilde, Askov Folk High School and Thyregod Free School, whose vacancy was to be filled in January 1904. I heard back by return of post from Hvalsømagle, who wished to see me for an interview, and from Thyregod Free School, who sent me a letter of appointment that same day, December 8. It turned out that Ervin had received a letter too that day – from Ryslinge, offering him a position in geography, history, and botany. He beamed with joy and felt sure that my not receiving any letter from them did not necessarily mean that they would not be sending a reply. It was quite conceivable that there would be several rounds of appointments, he said. I was happy on his behalf, but as for myself I had no idea what to think or do. The outcome was that I wrote to Thyregod's chairman, Peder Møllergaard, that same evening and accepted the appointment. I felt in no way that I could manage to cross the Storebælt in winter for an interview that would perhaps lead to nothing, for the letter from Hvalsømagle had said they would be calling four applicants to interview. Besides, Thyregod was offering an exceptionally good salary for a free-school teacher: 325 kroner plus free residence and fuel. We corresponded a couple of times as to the position and the district, how many children would be attending and so on. I asked what the surrounding area looked like. "The land is heathland," Peder Møllergaard replied. I hardly knew what heathland was at the time. But then, when everything was agreed and had fallen into place, I received a letter from Ryslinge Folk High School offering me a position in needlework, Danish, and physical education for girls. I said nothing to Ervin, not wishing to intervene in his joy at having secured his employment there. Perhaps he had also begun to think it best that I would be going to Thyregod.

Oddly, the letter was also dated December 8 and must have been mislaid at a post office for some days before being found and sent on. I wrote to tell my father and mother, and I discovered the draft of that letter the other day when I was rummaging in the bureau: "I am happy that everything has now been agreed with Thyregod Free School; the position there will be less burdensome and is better paid, and with that in mind it was not in the slightest bit difficult to turn them down at Ryslinge."

The truth of the matter is that it was difficult indeed to turn down a position at Ryslinge Folk High School. And what I did not tell my parents at the time was that I had done my utmost to engage Rasmus Laursen in helping me be released from my agreement with Thyregod. I wanted so much more to go to Ryslinge. But of course it was out of the question that he would be party to me leaving Thyregod in the lurch.

It is a dismal day. The thermometer by the kitchen doorstep shows two degrees Celsius. It is raining. I was at Rosenstand's grocery earlier on, and while I was there I heard there was a young doctor who was interested in taking over the practice. Apparently he was already on his way from Southern Jutland and received his training in Germany. People are already afraid they will not understand a word he says, but I said: "Think of Dr. Bagge. He was trained in Berlin, and you understood him well enough."

When I got home I went upstairs and opened the cupboards.

I do not know what to do with Vigand's clothes and books. It is not hard to imagine that people in these parts would be glad of his clothes at least, and have need of them too. But would I be able to cope with the sight of Viggo Hat sauntering along in Vigand's spring overcoat? Or to see his shoes on the feet of Jens Kristian Andersen?

What do you say, Vigand?

As ever, he has not the slightest doubt: "Oh, you'll get used to it," he says. No more than that, and no more is necessary. I believe him. Besides, I know him so well. If he were still alive, he would be amused at the thought of people in the town, people of no small means even, being envious of Terkelline's ragged son because of a pair of secondhand shoes. "You're wicked, Vigand," I tell him out loud, and suddenly it occurs to me that he cannot contradict me.

~

I took a room at the hotel in Strib the first night, then drove on the next morning to Ryslinge, where it turned out Ervin was still a teacher there. That lovely place. He has two daughters now, and a wife who is quite as cheerful and attentive and good-humored as he. She too is a teacher there. In fact, she told me she had been given the position they later learned had originally been offered to me, and she had always been thankful for me having turned it down and was glad to be able to tell me so now. I imagine one cannot be anything but cheerful with Ervin for a husband.

I felt like a stranger as I drove up to the main building in my car and Ervin himself came out onto the steps; a stranger also to myself, though Ervin is as fine as I remember him.

I stayed there the whole day, and Ervin's wife looked after me and was well-versed in our time at the School of Education. She was able to give me news of Erland too. He had started so well with a position at the folk high school at Ubberup, followed by marriage to a teacher there with whom he had three small girls, but seven or eight years ago he had caused a scandal by falling in love with one of his female students. It had ended in divorce, and Thit Jensen had raked him over the coals. An issue had been made of it in the newspapers, though somehow it had passed me by completely. And then, after all that, his relationship with the young woman had come to nothing and he had felt compelled to pack his bags and leave the school. "It was a shame for him," said Ervin's wife. It had been some time since they had last received word from him.

I attended the singing in the evening. The students sat or lounged on the benches with their arms draped around each other, some almost entwined, and the music teacher, whose evening off it was by rights, accompanied them on most any song they suggested. None of them wished to stop, myself included. We sang for what seemed like hours.

The next day, I went on to Faaborg. The poorhouse is no more. I knew, of course. But the tobacconist's on the corner still exists, albeit with new proprietors. One could buy soap there. I bought two bars with a rose-petal scent, and this afternoon I have written to Agnete and told her about the farm that now stands in the place of our childhood home. I have described it as a fine structure, and healthy to inhabit, for the main house is built of red brick, like so many others in recent years. I am quite certain they are not pestered by rats. But the old house was our home, cozy, orderly, and safe. I asked if she remembered Skipper, the poodle we once had;

our father fetched him as a puppy from Middelfart, and he grew up to be such a clever rat-catcher. Do you remember the two lime trees in the yard, Agnete? And the sound of the rain? And the red stone among the cobbles, that you said was yours?

I placed a bar of soap in the same envelope and wrote that I kept another for myself so that we might think of each other and know that we smelled alike.

~

Now I shall go upstairs and do something about Vigand's clothes.

November 23

I was thinking of that day in early January 1904 when I arrived with the train at Give. The railway ran no further at that time. With me I had a duffel bag and my bicycle, the rest of my things would be sent on. I had written to Peder Møllergaard saying that I intended to cycle the remainder of the way and had packed my bag accordingly so that it was no bigger than I could manage. When I left in the morning the weather had been fine, but as soon as we came to Vejle, where I had to change trains, the sky had become overcast and on the final half-hour of the way the air was a flurry of sleet. Grey-white globs darted past the window and there was hardly a tree in sight. Gusts of wind rocked the carriage.

At Give the platform was busy with people, mostly come to collect goods and parcels. My bicycle was lifted out and there I stood, blinded by wet snow. The station master took me in to sit by the tiled stove in the waiting room. He said: "There's always someone over from Thyregod to pick something up, and if all else fails you can go with the goods carrier. Wait here and I'll find out."

From upstairs came the sound of someone playing a piano, and a female voice sang: . . . *peep forth with petals small and white, that hearts may warm at such a sight*, and then, with emphatic and teacherly accentuation: *Then comes the lapwing!* Shortly afterwards, a little girl came skipping down the stairs, a roll of sheet music tucked under her arm, pulled open the door, and disappeared outside into the snow.

A short time passed before the door suddenly pushed open again and a big dog thrust its way in, bounded up to me and laid its head in my lap. Its eyes seemed to say: "There, I found you."

And so it had, I soon found out, because then a man came in, his hat and shoulders covered in snow, and said: "I told Bernhard to go in and find you."

"Then he's a very clever dog. If it was me he was meant to find, that is."

And indeed it was. We shook hands. His name was Peter Carlsen. It was the first time I saw him.

He put my bicycle in the back of his cart. He had come to pick up some lime, he said, and had been thinking that he could give me a lift. We got to know each other straight away. The dog sat calmly between us with Peter Carlsen's arm around it. "He likes you," he said.

"I like him too," I said, then suggested we dispense with the formal address: "By all means, use *du* rather than *De*," I said.

"I've heard it's customary at the folk high schools now," he said. "I'm all for it. *Du* it is, then."

The wind came sideways and before long I realized that I would not have been able to cycle at all. The road deteriorated as we went, the taller vegetation vanished completely and the wind picked up. "How nice and warm to have a dog," I shouted, and he shouted back and said yes, he was lucky that Bernhard liked to go out driving. We shuffled closer to the animal, which all the while sat bolt upright on the seat. He told me that he had always wanted the chance to attend a folk high school, but now at least they had managed to send his brother off. I asked if he had any children who would be going to the free school, but he told me he had none and that he was not yet married or even engaged, though he was very pleased the school had been founded. "It was rather a battle," he said. "Grundtvigians against the Inner Mission. It's all petered out now, though. Now we're happy about the school and happy we managed to secure your services."

"Thyregod in a minute," he said a couple of hours later. "Just down the hill here. On a clear day you can see it all, the church, the dairy, the mill. You'll be looking forward to getting yourself installed, I shouldn't wonder."

I asked him where he lived, and he said: "On the farm we passed a kilometer back."

I liked that. The fact that he had not pointed it out as we went by. There would have been plenty of time at the pace we were going. I understood he was not the sort who wished to impose himself.

It was dusk by the time we reached the school where I was to live and work.

∼

I have begun to pack, rather meticulously. At the grocery the other day, I asked Rosenstand if I might take any packing cases he no longer needs, and this morning he came by with eleven large ones and four smaller ones, with the promise of more to come. By way of thanks, I plied him with mid-morning coffee, which he sucked through a sugar lump. "But where are you intending to move?" he asked. I told him

I was unsure as yet, but that everything had to be packed regardless, and he could hardly disagree. He suggested I give Vigand's clothes to the Civic and Tradesmen's Association. They would know who was most in need, he said. So now the larger part is packed. Only his shirts still remain. I imagine that in a moment I shall tear them from their hangers and hurl them into the case with the rest of his clothes, so that I may understand once and for all that his smell is no longer for me. That it has gone with him. Vigand would applaud it, if he could.

My thoughts at present are on what it means to have a home. There must be a roof over one's head, shelter and warmth, but these are of course not the only requirements. Terkelline Andersen refused to vacate her decrepit, broken-down house when the parish council wished to install her somewhere else, and declared that she wanted to die in her own home. And her son lives there still, though in his case perhaps feelings are the least of it. At any rate, I have heard it said that he would be quite as happy in a foxhole. How anyone would know is beyond me – certainly he will not have said a word himself. He is not the communicative kind. He was here yesterday as well, just after the grocer Rosenstand left, selling rubber bands. There was still some coffee in the pot, and I asked him to come in and sat him down on the bench in the kitchen. His face is crimson red and troubled, and most of the time he sits staring at the floor, but suddenly, and this has always been his way, he will lift his gaze and his eyes will be piercing and firm. When I was young and new here, he frightened me many a time with that look. He was not in the habit of knocking and would walk straight in. He would leave his wooden shoes in the passage and I would not hear him until he was standing in the living room. He could come in the early mornings and after school at any time in the evening, and it was because of him that I began to lock my door. The folk were unaccustomed to it. In these parts they lock their houses only when going out, and even then they leave the key in the door so that visitors should not come in vain to the step. Once, I had fallen asleep with my arms over the table in the kitchen, and all of a sudden I felt a hand pass over my hair, gently and with great caution, and when I opened my eyes and looked up he was standing there with his ruddy cheeks and big red beard. They called him Petting-Jens in those days. On another occasion, I discovered an unplucked drake dangling from my door handle. It had been dead for some time and looked rather seedy to say the least. There was no shot in it, nor any sign of such, and I knew it could only be from him. Not that he wished to frighten me, but because he genuinely believed he could make an impression by wringing the neck of a duck, and that I would find it delicate and inviting. I took a spade from the outhouse and buried it in the yard immediately.

In the beginning I repressed my sense of unease, believing that I should present myself as hospitable and without prejudice. Occasionally, I would offer him coffee, if only for the chance to tell him that he ought to wash himself and get his hair cut, but he never took the slightest notice and it would feel awkward to have him sit there and stare at me, and moreover tongues began to wag, people said he had taken a fancy to the free-school mistress and had even been inside her chamber, which was true enough, but not the way they thought, and so I put an end to it. After that he shut himself away for years and has only recently ventured out again. We have never spoken properly. Yet he is capable of the oddest things. Today, he quoted from *Terje Vigen*:

> *There lived a remarkably grizzled man*
> *on the uttermost, barren isle*
> *he never harmed, in the wide world's span,*

a soul by deceit or by guile;
his eyes, though, sometimes would blaze and fret
most when a storm was nigh,
and then people sensed he was troubled yet
and then there were few that felt no threat
with Terje Vigen by.

Nevertheless, it was no comfortable sitting, and he mumbles as well and is therefore hard to understand. However, I gathered it was Ibsen and asked him how he knew it. He told me it was from reading. I bought ten rubber bands from him and hope that the Civic and Tradesmen's Association will provide him with a good pair of trousers. I felt no compulsion to do so myself.

～

When that evening we turned up Nørregade we came again into the open land. "There it is, Frøken Høy," said Peter Carlsen, pointing into the flurrying snow. He brought the horses to a standstill and helped me down. Lifted my bicycle from the back. I asked if I might offer him coffee, but he had to be getting home to tend to the livestock, and I happened to think of what a detour he had made in order to take me all the way to the town. He placed a key in my hand. "Peder Møllergaard sends his regards. He wanted to be here to bid you welcome, but he'll be over tomorrow. Are you going to be all right?"

I stepped into a hallway and opened a door on the right which turned out to lead into the schoolroom. There was a lamp on the teacher's desk, which I managed to light. I was so anxious to see what awaited me. The schoolroom with its desks and blackboard, the round, black tiled stove and the peat box. A tall, glass-fronted cupboard with reading books and songbooks in it, and on the wall a series of educational posters depicting family life, peat-cutting and autumnal ploughing. A picture of a city, and one of winter. Varnished floorboards and three very large windows, through which the light would pour in the daytime. Yes, I was most happy with what I saw. In the hallway from where I had come, the floor was tiled, and therefore easily mopped, and on the walls there were coat hooks and twenty cubby holes containing twenty new pairs of small cloth slippers, one pair in each. From the hallway a door leading off into the teacher's accommodation on the other side, and a steep flight of steps to the loft. My rooms were at the end of the house. There was a kitchen with a great chimney and a stove far too big for one person, moreover a living room with a table, chairs, a bookcase, and an armchair. A small chamber with a bed, a night table and a chair. Apart from the stove, everything was better than I had allowed myself to hope for. The rooms had been heated up during the day. The fire had gone out now, but my father had given me kindling to take with me, which accounted for most of the contents of my duffel bag. I put the schoolroom lamp in the window, thinking that if anyone should come past they would find the place inviting, this January evening on Nør-regade. The wind battered the house, but it was solidy built of brick. I put my books in the cupboard in the schoolroom and ate the rest of the packed lunch I had brought with me. There was a smell of fresh woodwork, everything was brand new and ready.

Thinking back, I almost feel envious of that young school-mistress. In fact, there is no almost about it.

~

Now and then, it seems as if I *want* to fall into a trap. I lay awake last night and felt so embittered. For long periods of time I am able to remind myself to contain the bitterness of my private life so as not to lose my dignity or narrow my horizons. I know people who can only talk about what has gone wrong and who complain about the offenses caused by others to such an extent that one wishes it were possible to cover one's ears and run away as one sits there nodding and smiling and trying to lead the conversation in some other direction, and to at least interest them in a piece of cake. But in my darkest moments I understand only too well the kind of misfortune that can leave a person in such a place. Bitterness is a very soft and comfortable armchair from which it is difficult indeed to extract oneself once one has decided to settle in it.

Why was I not allowed to help you when you were dying, Vigand?

Why did you not answer my letter?

His voice, so seldom hesitant, says nothing. I tossed and turned in the bed, until eventually I got up and went downstairs, though I did not light the lamp. That silence, it betrays me.

November 25

To begin with, the children sat and stared at me. There was not a thing to complain about as regards discipline, one could hear a pin drop, but their silence had me bewildered, until it struck me that perhaps it was my Fyn-land accent that was so unfamiliar to them they thought it to be some kind of foreign language.

"Can you understand what I say?" I asked.

"No," said a girl.

"Then we must sing," I said.

We sang our way through the days in that early time. They came from the municipal school where they had learned only the Mission hymns, so they were completely unfamiliar with the likes of *Fano, Mano and Romo* or *Once in Olden Days*. They were a lot less humble after they learned that they were to address me using the *du* form and were not required to spring to their feet when I asked them a question, that we would not be using the cane, and that moreover I encouraged them to ask if there was anything they didn't understand. "Aren't you going to be cross soon?" they asked, but it was quite unnecessary.

As in all free schools, we began each day with a hymn, the Lord's Prayer, and then another hymn. We sang in every lesson. Immediately after morning song we had storytelling, where I told them stories from the Bible or Danish history, about the siege of Copenhagen, about Svend Gønge and Svend Trøst, Cain and Abel, or Hamlet, Prince of Denmark. The children made drawings as they listened, and were very fond of it. Afterwards came arithmetic and spelling, and we would chorus the rhymes: B A says ba, B U says bu, B Æ says bæ. But otherwise learning by rote was not allowed. Some of the parents were puzzled by this and feared their children would not be confirmed if they were unable to recite the Ten Commandments and hymns from memory, and there were even a few who took their children out of the school when it was rumored what kind of teaching I practiced. I had several discussions with Peder Møllergaard, who impressed upon me that there was a balance that needed to be kept at all times.

I was fond of those children. I think they were fond of me, too. In an unremarkable kind of way. Only once did anything like deep-felt affection come to expression. It was after a lesson when little Ludvig Ludvigsen asked me to bend forward, and when I did he smoothed his hand over my hair and ran out through the door leaving me astonished and rather overwhelmed at my desk. And when I think about it now, it astonishes me still. Was it something he had been intending to do, or did he just do it? If he were here now, I should like to ask him.

Yes, everything seemed so easy to me. But even in that regard there was a balance to be kept. And it was up to me to keep it. Once, in exuberance at the children's proficiency and eagerness to learn, I found myself saying to them as we were about to have dictation that anyone with more than seven mistakes would have their ears boxed. None of them ever had more than seven mistakes, and I considered it a joy to be relished by us all that in our school no one would ever be physically punished in any circumstance, not even if the teacher were strict or unfair. I think I wanted to show the children that if the teacher or another adult were ever unfair, another, stronger kind of justice would prevail, and that they were protected by it. But on that day it was as if a fly were buzzing about inside my head, I reached out and snatched it the way I snatched at others that would lead us off into spelling games on the blackboard or physical exercises in the aisle when the weather would not permit us to go outside.

The children were so anxious that over half the class, from the brightest to the dullest, had more than seven mistakes. I was unable to go back on what I had said. In the deepest silence, I went from desk to desk and boxed their ears. I was as gentle as could be: first I smoothed my hand over their cheeks as if to take the sting from what I was about to do, and to make them understand that I didn't mean it, and then I boxed their ears. I did not hit them hard, but still little Ludvig Ludvigsen fell weeping over his desk, as did several of the girls. At the time, I did not know that love and violence from the same hand is more fear-inducing than violence on its own.

The first thing I did in the morning was light the stove in the schoolroom. Because the peat contained so much sand, the ash pan had to be emptied daily. I teetered outside with it and the chamber pot, my hair but loosely plaited, in my dressing gown and wooden shoes, to the rear of the building where the schoolmistress's washroom was situated. It was quite an expedition in rain and wind and slush, and I was glad the school was secluded. The nearest neighbor was a hundred meters away. Once I had washed and dressed, I wiped the desks and the window sills and mopped the floor. It was the sort of job I ought properly to have done in the evenings, but normally I was so tired after evening classes and the lecture society and the sports association and whatever else that kept me occupied, that all I could manage was to go home and go straight to bed. I wanted the place to smell fresh when the children came. I wanted it to be a cozy place in which they felt comfortable. We had geraniums in the window, for they too had been in my duffel bag when I arrived: four little cuttings wrapped in wet newspaper. I entrusted the children with looking after them. Indeed, they helped me with as much as they could. The boys carried water in, so I never needed to carry a full bucket, and they filled the peat box for me too, in my rooms as well as the schoolroom.

When the children arrived at eight o'clock the place was nice and warm. They came trudging in their wooden shoes that were heavy with the mud and snow they had picked up along the way, and their legs were often wet to the knee. Many of them lived a long way from the school and had already been hard at work for some time. I kept a good stock of dry socks. Every day, their wet ones would be hung to dry at the stove. They loved to put their dry socks and slippers on before we started. We kept a pot of milk on the stove too, so they could get some warmth inside them. I felt privileged indeed. Sometimes, in the privacy of my mind, I thought of them as own.

All the children I have known are long since grown up. Perhaps because I was only a teacher for such a short time, I remember each and every one so distinctly, and when occasionally during the many years I lived in Give I happened to see one of them, their names would pop from my lips and I would stop in my tracks and clap my hands together with glee. It was not that I tended to think about them ordinarily, but seeing them would call attention to a longing I until then hardly knew was there. After Vigand moved his practice to Thyregod, I have naturally seen them more often. The girls come and show me their babies whenever they give birth, and I can tell that my interest brings them joy. But only a few years from now they will reach the grandmothering age, for in these parts the women start early. The boys work hard. They all work hard. If truth be told, they have little in common with the children they once were. Some of them are dead. Little Ludvig Ludvigsen perished from some peculiar seizure, Jens Thiis fell from the barn loft, and Madeleine Kristoffersen and Jens Jensen died in the Spanish flu epidemic in 1918. Oscar Vestergaard disappeared. Of twenty-two children, five are already no more.

Such shifting winds in life. Therein the advantage of becoming older. One finds oneself with several lives, and may skip from one to another. Every so often it feels like I remember it all. Most probably I cannot.

~

The first spring I was there, the children had somehow discovered it was my birthday, and there I was thinking that I would surprise them: I had baked a cake that we were going to share during the lunch break. Only then it turned out they had brought me something. A handful of one and two-øre coins. It was so very seldom that folk had money in their hands. At the grocer's they bartered for their groceries with eggs and meat, and apart from that most tended to be self-sufficient. "How on earth have you managed to save up such a sum?" I exclaimed, and they laughed secretively and asked me if I had ever seen so much money before. They asked as well what I would like to buy.

I went to Hansen's grocery. His business is substantial now, as it was becoming then, situated in the old yard with timber stock and stables and storehouses. I had a notion that I might buy myself a blouse, but instead my attention was caught by the paraffin lamp that once again this evening burns in my window. It is such a fine lamp, with its round, frosted dome and brass base.

"Look what I've bought with your money," I said when I showed them the lamp the next day. "I shall put it in the window in the evenings so that people can see it from the road when they come past." They thought it was fine. Oscar Vestergaard said: *"But y'wid nae a' had eneugh?"* I told him I had chipped in. Later, I overheard him say to some men standing by the skittle alley: *"She shewed us a lamp she'd bot wee t'munny, but she sayed t'wus nae eneugh."*

The inn was my nearest neighbor. At that time it adjoined Vester Farm, which has since been moved up the hill here. A great, filthy muck heap lay outside by the road along with all manner of rubbish and refuse that blew across the field in any decent wind. When spring came, the noises from the skittle alley drifted over to the school, the sudden shouts and cries. Alcohol was swilled, and scraps were commonplace.

Jens Kristian Andersen sometimes came to my door before going over there and would confide to me that he did not feel at ease in the place. And yet he went. When there was money in his pocket, the others would talk to him, but otherwise they treated him abominably. I have seen him so drunk that his face was completely benumbed, his eyes empty and dead, glazed with fever. I have seen him in that state many a time. And not only him.

It caused a certain stir when I came to the town. There was the bicycle, for one thing, and then the fact that I was a woman and on my own, and moreover a trained teacher. I think it may safely be said that to the young men, or perhaps the men in general, I was an attractive blend of something attainable and yet absolutely unattainable. One of my more singular admirers was the miller, who also earned a living tarring roofs. One day, when he was at work on the dairy roof, the sight of me walking along the road prompted him to do a handstand on the roof ridge and wave his legs about. He was an old man then. At least ten years older than I am now. Later, he fell from the church tower without hurting himself. Nevertheless, he ended up an invalid after a fall. His wife opened a hair salon and they lived on the income she made. People were resourceful in Thyregod. Resourceful and strong-willed.

It was a very small town. I am not sure it even merited the word. In the town itself, besides the mill and the church, the inn and the dairy, and the grocer Hansen's yard, Vester Farm and the free school, there was almost nothing but Line's little emporium, which sold nearly anything one can imagine and would later boast a public telephone, and a couple of miserable houses belonging to poor folk. But there were street lamps. Every evening, the tobacconist would hang oil lamps up on their posts with a long pole.

Surrounding the town was the heath.

I have seen the sandy earth shift after the spring sowing. The sky was as black as Doomsday. The sand crept in everywhere, and deposited itself in drifts on the floors of my rooms. To be out in such a storm is inconceivable, people die from it. Machinery becomes blanketed, livestock succumb. And people's despair at the perished seed, that too I have seen.

I have seen the heath. It is nearly all gone now. I have seen the fires when it was burned off to be cultivated. The smoke drifted chokingly across the land, a low mantle above the ground. When the flames caught it was like a sea suddenly rising up, its thunderous waves were yellow and wild, and ahead of them leapt the hares, the partridges scuttled, and black grouse flapped into the air, adders and grass snakes slithered, here and there a fox emerged. And then they were engulfed. The fires went on for hours. In the night, men watched over them. And when morning came, the charred corpses were revealed.

Now Vigand makes himself known: "A true witness of truth," he remarks in that oddly spurious voice he has occasionally employed of late.

I think I shall go for a drive in the dark. I shall proceed slowly along the road, and see who might be out.

November 27

We were married for twenty-two years, and although it has been a time in which many things have happened – a world war, motor cars, electricity, women's suffrage – indeed an entire world would seem to have wound down and been replaced by a new one, I would still venture that those years have been one long and unbroken day.

For me it has been a quiet time.

November 28

The butcher Schnedler has done up his window for Christmas. Two pigs with pixie hats on and cob pipes inserted between their discolored teeth have been seated on a bench. Their bare hocks and trotters poke towards the beholder as if they were stretching their muscles. It looks so very human, and draws as much attention as ever. The children gather to watch the butcher and his wife manhandle the pigs onto the bench, where they are tied to the backrest with a rope around the midriff. Scarves are wrapped around their necks and arranged to cover their sliced bellies, concealing their horrible plight, and finally Fru Schnedler inserts the pipes into their mouths and puts their hats on. They look like they are having a fine time on their bench, in the midst of a good gossip.

Today I was on my way in the car to ask Dagmar and Inge if they would care for a spin, but on the way up the hill to Hedebjerg Farm it began to rain and I ended up driving past. Often I feel silly in that car. Such a noisy spectacle. What do I even need it for, other than to make a show of myself?

During the singing at Ryslinge Folk High School, among all the young people who are so wrapped up in each other as to think of nothing but living, one finds little reason to ask questions of oneself. One may sing anything at all, even the glummest of songs, without feeling anything other than joy. Song and blood are so very much alike, they flow through us. Now too, as I pick up the Folk High School Song Book and sing for myself in a voice so feeble it would seem to be afraid of the room here, it will flow if only I raise myself.

> *The bright sun starts to set, soon evening will be here,*
> *Each laborer is tired and hopes that rest is near:*
> *To death I am yet one day closer than before,*
> *Time for me*
> *Unhurriedly*
> *Is opening death's door.*

Yes. Death is often a matter for one rather than two, as I had wished it. Was Vigand so by himself, I wonder? Or did he die in self-defense against me?

Can a radical perdition be entertained? The idea of a human life without value?

November 30

In my employment as a free-school teacher, the children were by no means my only occupation. A new time had begun, and I was young and vigorous, with a head full of ideas and rooms in which they could be realized. After school the girls would come back for sewing lessons. There were so many that I had to take them in groups by turn, since I used my own private living room where we were able to sit more comfortably. They received instructions to wash their hands thoroughly. As they sewed, I would read aloud to them, albeit with many interruptions, for my own needle-work required attention too whenever it went wrong, as it so often did. The evenings were taken by various activities. I taught physical exercise in the temperance hotel's function room, and in the winter season there were parents' meetings once a week. These were not meetings at which the children were discussed, but assemblies for the debate of important topics – much in the way of a folk high school, though of course on a smaller scale. Sometimes there would be read-ings, and I would have boxes of books sent over from the library in Vejle for people to borrow. Occasionally, we would arrange a dance so that people would not have to go to the inn. We organized a lecture society too, and invited speakers from outside. Often they would be teachers and clergymen from the neighboring parishes. The subjects were many and varied: the folk-high-school movement, the co-operative movement, the plantation movement, kitchen gardens, fruit growing, the need for a health commission. I wrote to Vigand and asked if he might come and speak to us one evening, and he came and talked about hygiene in the kitchen, the perils of preparing food with dirty hands in dirty pots and pans, and the kind of individuals born from the mealy white sauce most of them consumed every day of the year. He spoke too of the importance of letting fresh air into the home. I have no recollection of his personality that evening. He was the remote physician. I am sure that I welcomed him as best I could.

On such evenings, when something was going on at the school, I had much to do making coffee and buttering bread. In most cases, some wives came over and helped.

I received no compensation for these extra-curricular activities, and Peder Møllergaard, aware of how hard stretched I was, particularly in periods when the parents had insufficient surplus to supply me with peat or eggs, arranged for me to be given a small job as district singer for Thyregod and Vester churches. It was not a regular position, but I would be called upon in cases of urgent baptism as well as for funerals. I also sang at weddings.

~

Today, the grocer Rosenstand was here with his van to collect the packing cases I have filled. He took the beds from the bedroom, and the dresser and the bedside tables while he was at it, and asked me to let him know if there was anything else. He told me he would have no trouble finding people who would make good use of whatever I no longer needed. I cleaned the windows, brushed down the cobwebs, and mopped the floor after he was gone. Now I need never go in there again.

December 1

Line's room has now been emptied and cleaned as well, and with Hilda's help the scullery and the cellar are both in the process. Although we have only lived here for eight years, things have accummulated. All the jam that was made and forgotten about has been donated to the Christmas bazaar at the Mission Hotel. We carried seven boxes full up the stair. Eggs in waterglass, years old, were thrown out; Hilda thought it a shame, but when I asked her if she wanted them she nonetheless declined. It was quite a job extracting them from their jars, the waterglass was like stone. We took them outside and pelted the birch, the garden's only tree as such. Smack, smack, smack. They smelled dreadful and rotten, but we became so absorbed that we carried on until not a single egg was left. Hilda, who is tiny and worn to the bone, had to stand up close to the tree, since her arms cannot throw very far. Every joint in her body aches, but it is plain to see that there once was something she loved. Work, perhaps. Afterwards, we had coffee and her *lapper* cakes.

She asked me where I was going to live, and when I told her

I had no idea, she cautiously suggested that I had better find out. She is not the only one to think so. Peder Møllergaard came yesterday, and with him the young doctor people have been talking about of late. They were here to see the consultation, but wished to pay their regards first. I found him pleasant and appealing. He is exactly as I imagined. Young. Engaged to be married. He almost gasped with delight when he stepped into the study and saw Vigand's deep armchair and the bookshelves. When I came back in with the coffee tray, I found him standing there perusing the volumes. They did not stay long. I took them around the outside to the consultation after coffee.

It is afternoon and the air is clear, the final light is dwindling. It is just past four o'clock.

~

And now evening again. Each day draws with it the next. Such a difference there is between day and evening. In the evenings, secret friends come scampering. Old joys, old sorrows, and all that lies between. They come with the light. I strike a match and put it to the wick of the lamp. Peace fills the room, and fills me too.

This afternoon, while out walking, I came by Rose Cottage, and as the light was failing and there was nobody around I entered the garden. It is a large garden, slightly more than an acre, I would say. One part is given over to fruit, another to flowers, a third to vegetables. There is an abandoned hen-house, which I inspected. The door was a job to open. Inside smelled of rotten straw, and the roost was thick with dried excrement, quite as malodorous. I peered in at all the windows of the house, or those I could reach, which made me feel so oddly ill at ease that I walked back the long way, stopping at the rectory where Fru Grell was standing in the kitchen, her cheeks glistening as she was making black pudding. It was a comforting sight; it reminded me that everything is still there. I am not sure what I mean by that exactly. And yet: Vigand is dead, and there is more that I cannot hope to even approach, but the practical things remain, which is good. The practical life, black pudding and the light of industry in a kitchen, is so very good indeed. She told me about a new reading group she would like to begin after Christmas and asked if I would care to join. I told her I would. She came out to the step with me when I left. The wind rushed in the trees at the bottom of the garden, and we stood for a moment and listened. She does the same each evening, she told me. She is fond of the sound.

I am too.

Now, with the time at twenty past eight, I feel companionless. My peace is gone, and my secret friends with it. Only solitude remains. It cannot bear to be with others. Never, never will you find attachment to your life, it whispers. You are bound to be a stranger who knows not what to do. Get out, I tell it emphatically. Get out!

～

I shall leave the books for the new doctor. Perhaps he will find some of them useful, and he should have no trouble disposing of the rest.

December 3

I used to walk past Rose Cottage almost daily. It was my favorite walk, there being a garden there with trees in it. An old man lived there at the time, Peder Pedersen, who used to have the farm at Herthasminde, and after planting there he bought Rose Cottage instead, as the place to pass his old age, and planted the garden there too. Now and again when I came past he would invite me inside the gate. Once, he gave me a full-blown sprig of jasmin, which I took home with me and which filled the schoolroom with such a sweet and luxuriant smell of summer it almost brought tears to my eyes. I have always been fond of flowers, though quite how fond I had no idea until I came here, where there were none. And yet, that is not entirely true. Our Lady's bedstraw, for instance, on a sun-warmed slope, with wild thyme in bloom. No fragrance is as balmy. And the globeflowers too. But I was sorry about the bare schoolyard, whose grass was scuffed away under the children's feet and whittled down by the stiff and foul-tempered wind that came at us from the west, for there was nothing there to stop it. I wished for an educational garden and a place where the children could learn the joys of planting and watch things grow, and most of all I wished for shelter from the wind. When spring came again, my second in Thyregod, I spoke to Peder Møllergaard about it. He told me I should have a word with Peter Carlsen. "Have you seen what he's done?" he asked. "At Hedebjerg Farm?"

I said no, I hadn't.

"Then putting myself in your place I'd go and have a look," he said. "I think you'll find it interesting. And you'll enjoy the walk, I know."

Some time afterwards he returned to the matter. He asked if I had been there yet. I said no, that I had been too tied up with things to do.

"Then putting myself in your place I'd go tomorrow," he said. "I happen to know there's nothing to keep you."

It was rather surprising. Twice he had said "putting myself in your place." I remember it puzzled me, as it would anyone else who knew Peder Møllergaard, whose stout-heartedness was legend, for although he would take care of things for people, unravel their knots so as to allow them to get on with their lives, he was not a person who tended to put himself in the place of others. He was a leader. It felt like he was giving me a shove. But I wanted to go anyway.

I took the bicycle that day, though generally it was often more of a hindrance than a help. I kept having to get off and walk, long stretches of track where I almost had to drag it along. But I was fond of that bicycle. One sat so proudly on it. I have it still, and it is quite as good as before, despite having been used almost daily.

Peter Carlsen's mother was out in the yard in front of the house, picking weeds in a bucket. I remember her straightening up a little and resting her elbows on her thighs when I came. "*Nae, wod a neece s'prise*," she said. Such a smile on her face. I cannot say that it was anything else but a smile, but it was a smile that said so much about the person. And her eyes, like stable windows. Often I have seen old people bent almost double and yet engaged in conversation, elbows on knees, hands paused in whatever they happened to be doing when they were interrupted. They look as if they have all the time in the world, when the fact of the matter is that their bodies ache and they are unable to draw themselves up. It is a sight so peculiarly full of grace.

How can I say that Carl resembles his grandmother? They are so very different. She had the happiest face, the happiest eyes. Perhaps it is merely a charming appeal they share, with no other similarity?

He was here today, shortly before twelve. I had just set the table for myself and was about to tuck into a slice of liver and two potatoes when there was a knock on the door. I was glad of the company. He wanted nothing to eat, only to show me his photographs. We cleared the things aside and sat down at the kitchen table, the kitchen being the only room that was properly warm, and he took them from an envelope one by one and pointed out the various motives with a finger whose nail was bitten to the quick. His hands have always been clean, as opposed to most other boys I have known. When he was little he used to want to wash them all the time. Now it seems as if he is down to the red flesh. He explained to me how he develops and makes copies of his photographs. He closes the shutter at the window and uses a torch with red paper in front of the bulb. The photographs themselves are sepia-colored and very small. He calls them daylight prints and tells me they are quite perishable. I had to put my glasses on and pick them up to be able to see them properly. He photographs everything with the same enthusiasm. Borgergade, Grundtvigs Plads, his sisters shelling peas on a doorstep, the reaper-binder, his father forking hay, the chimney at the dairy, his sisters no longer shelling peas on a doorstep. "Carl," I said, "this is a treasure trove." There were two I recognized. Johannes V. Jensen's wife standing in front of the French doors at the hotel in Give. She is insignificant in the photograph, whereas a flower arrangement and a table-edge leap out. But still I stared at it for some time. The other is of Hilda and me in the car that day by the station. How very different I look compared to how I imagined. So much in charge. Perhaps it is the hat I was wearing. But Hilda looked the same as ever.

"Have you eaten the apples?" Carl asked.

"I forgot," I said with regret.

He nodded and said: "Maglemer Stripling's a dull apple."

"How are Dagmar and Inge?" I asked.

"They're fine," he said.

"How's your father?"

"He's fine," he said.

Before he left he photographed the gramophone, and me sitting on the sofa.

One can wonder where his charm lies. Perhaps in the very fact of him coming to see me. The fact that he finds me interesting enough to come. I am sure that like me he is unaware of exactly what he is looking for, and that is the nice thing about it.

It feels like everything is the same. I get up in the mornings and drink my tea. I stare at the light in the garden, if there is light at all that day. I stare into the branches of the birch. I tidy up. People come and go, and box after box is carried from the house. There are no divisions, not even between what happened and what happens, and if that is untrue it is because I cannot remember for the moment. Everything has been erased. Only by some effort do I recall how lonely I was yesterday. Today I am not.

December 4

I keep thinking of Peter Carlsen's mother, her stable-window eyes, and then it occurs to me that at the gable-end there was a holly taller than me, dark and shiny and substantial.

"How can it grow here?" I asked.

"I've watched it grow," she replied. "I brought it home myself, in the pocket of my apron, when it was only so big."

She told me that she and her sisters had been visiting an aunt over in Kølkær one time when they were children, a near thirty-kilometer hike, and that they had taken a twig back with them. She broke one off and gave it to me, and said that I should plant it by the school. In sixty years time it would be just as big.

I feel the urge to stop by and see if it is still there. After the free school closed, the building housed an elementary school and then a vocational school, but ten years have passed now since the place was sold and turned into a private dwelling. I never saw the holly grow.

I have begun to pack my own things now. The whole house here is gradually resembling a storage room, and I have no need to ask Rosenstand for any more packing cases. He is a daily visitor, bringing the empty boxes in person rather than sending his messenger, and with opinions as to which are most suited for a particular item. We have coffee in the kitchen. Sometimes he comes twice a day. I have the impression he can hardly wait to empty his boxes so that he can return them to me, and I cannot imagine anything other than that he must need them himself. He has an opinion on many matters. It feels strange to suddenly be inviting him in. I have known him for a good number of years and have always found it pleasant to be a customer of his; he has always presented himself as a person of insight and manners, perhaps because our conversations have been confined to coffee and raisins, but for the last few days he has reminded me of something else. A dog perhaps. I am afraid that very soon he will jump up at me. In which case I intend to brush him off and send him home. He has been widowed four years now, and it is plain that he would like to be married again. How can he imagine that I might be interested in that? It makes me embarrassed on his behalf. He courts me with packing cases, the nice man. And of course I need them, which makes the whole arrangement rather awkward.

"But surely you haven't the time to sit here drinking coffee?" I say to him.

"Oh, business is well in hand," he replies, and asks for another cup. Usually, I must begin to clear the table before he thinks it time to be getting on.

He finds it odd that I still do not know where I am going to live. Odd, and no doubt ridiculous, considering how purposeful my endeavors are to pack.

I am afraid to think about it. When I peered in at the windows of Rose Cottage the day before yesterday, the cobwebs were thick and of the kind that are laden with eggs, and the wooden floor in the living room was stained dark in the middle, as if some great pot had been spilt, or something else had seeped through the floorboards for a considerable time.

I think he believes me to be in need of a man, a path and a direction in which to proceed.

I stood with my books. Over the years I have put things away in them. Four-leafed clovers and anaemic blooms whose species I have been unable to determine. A note containing only a few words, with no indication of its sender. In all this time, I have known it was there, but I have not looked at it, nor in fact do I look at it now.

I found a portrait of Vigand too, taken at Appel's the photographers in Give. His waistcoat is buttoned to the neck. He is sporting a full beard, half-spectacles, hat and cane. At first blush he looks like an old man, but his skin is young. It was taken just when he began as district physician, ten years before he made me a present of it. He is thirty-five years old. I was fifteen at the time. Perhaps he was engaged to someone and had his photograph taken for their benefit. His handwriting is on the back: *From V. Bagger, District Physician, June 1, 1905.* Three weeks later we were married. And now I cannot rid myself of the thought of that other young woman, the one he ought to have had instead. I imagine her to have been dark-haired, slim, wealthy and above all intelligent. In all the many years we were married, I have always so clearly imagined another woman as to be able to see her features. Thus, I feel certain that her nose was long and narrow, that her cheekbones were high and prominent, her eyes big and perceptive, and grey in color. But Vigand never spoke of another, and never commended any other woman but Fru Andersen. And we, we were married in a storm.

~

I have seen the young doctor's fiancée. He thought she ought to view the place, and they came and said hello. I made them coffee and we sat in the bay window. I asked her if she would like to see the house, and she saw it all, even the wash-house, even the boiler tub. She looks young, and in fact I think of her as a child. But what was I like myself, I wonder, when I was her age? I was strong, definitely. And I knew everything, probably more than I know now.

With age comes a certain naivety. Perhaps we no longer can bear the things we know and must smooth them away, leveling ourselves in the process. The differences we even out are evened out by human hand. The very old say so very little, not because they are unable, but because they cannot be bothered.

I asked her if the matter was decided, and she said: "I hope so." She seems a pleasant and considerate sort, much as her pleasant and considerate man, and it was no fault of hers that she could not conceal her contentment at the sight of my packing cases, but rather because I can be as hard as nails when the mood strikes me.

The living room is still cozy. The sofa is still there, and the armchairs and the bureau. The lamp in the window. Lit now, since the evening has come. For the first time in days, I have been outside on the step and felt the air. There is a coldness on its way. A stillness.

When it comes to Peter Carlsen, the following is to be remarked: Nothing had been said, and nothing had been done. He was my secret friend, so secret that even I was unknowing. There was a joy shut tight inside me. One could hardly have called it a hope. It was a joy, greater than joy itself.

Perhaps, if I had been taken on at Ryslinge, the same might have happened with Ervin.

~

His mother said that Peter was in Brande and had taken the dog with him, and that they would not be home until evening. She showed me the orchard. There were rows of young trees, apple and pear, plum and cherry. They were so slender and slight it moved my heart. She told me they had been there four years, and I thought of Fyn, where an apple tree planted four years ago would be taller than me. Every year they replanted, she said: "He plants all year round. Ever since he was a boy, all he's ever thought about is planting. He learned it from Peder Pedersen from Herthasminde. And from Dalgas." And it is true. Whenever one passes by Hedebjerg Farm, with its long avenue of chestnut, the orchards, the hedgerows, the thickets in the fields giving shelter to the game, the garden with its windbreak of tall trees, one understands that the farm, which originally grew up out of the heath, owes its present form entirely to a vision. No amount of hard work is ever sufficient in itself.

At one point the housekeeper appeared with the washing. She came and shook hands and was very nice. Her name was Henriette. She told me she had been on the farm some eighteen months and that she would soon be going home, albeit reluctantly. Then she laughed and put her arm under the old woman's. "She's my mother's sister," she said, "but she could just as well be my mother." The old woman patted her hand. How old was she? About thirty, I think. Her face was heavy and good.

They would mention to Peter Carlsen that I had been to see him, but I think they forgot. It was the sowing season, a busy time.

Rose Cottage, February 5, 1928

This morning the light streamed in through the living room window. I have fallen into the habit of eating breakfast on the sofa, since from there one may look out directly into the garden. The stretching view. Halfway to the orchard there is a squint little spruce that I immediately decided I did not care for, and I told Carl I wanted it removed. But then he showed me how to smear the branches with fat and sprinkle them with seeds, and now every day is a field day for the sparrows. The little tree looks like it has come alive. It shivers and shudders, and wings poke out from it all over. Such a lot of chirping. Occasionally it verges on commotion. I have stolen a march on spring.

But snow lies on the ground in its fourth week, and the car is covered up with horse blankets. Since driving it up here I have not been out in it a single time. It was an unpleasant drive. The tires are not much wider than a bicycle's, and I had no sense at all of being able to steer. Only by luck did it eventually get parked.

The last couple of months have been busy and good.

Thorsen, the decorator, has wallpapered and painted and whitewashed, and laid new carpets throughout. The money has flown like great flocks of starlings from my hands. Such fun it has been. The outhouses have been repaired, and Hilda and I have washed and scrubbed from end to end. When all was done, we went through the house together, and she squeezed both my hands and declared: "Fru Bagge is a lady."

Indeed. Everything here is arranged for my convenience, and mine alone. In the kitchen, there is a small table so that I may eat there without feeling a lack of company, for there is room for only one. In the bedroom, one bed without any tall end-boards to pen me in. I had Thorsen paint the room pale blue and put up a roller blind. There is an armchair for me to sit in, and the light falls on the dresser. I am already fond of every room. Each has something about it that attaches me to it: light or a curtain or an inviting nook in which to sit. The bookcase contains my books only. Vigand did not read fiction. I left his armchair behind in the study of the doctor's residence.

It occurred to me that Rosenstand should have his boxes back. The daily visits continue, now in his car, since at Christmas time he purchased a Benz and has driven about in it ever since. He has seen the entire house and uttered knowledge-able and complimentary words about most of it, though he then considered that the tiled stoves lacked proper ventila-tion and made improvements accordingly. Now he comes every day to inspect and make sure they work. In return I am naturally compelled to offer him coffee. I know that he is making it all up, and yet I cannot bring myself to suggest that I have seen through him. It makes me embarrassed on his behalf that he should think me so stupid.

Today he drove into the ditch and turned the car on its side in front of the house. I ran out to help, but he would hear none of it and managed to bring it upright again on his own. He revved the engine to get the vehicle back on the road, but it would hardly budge. Several times he climbed out to peer under the bonnet; eventually he asked for a spade and dug the wheels free at the front and back, though to no avail. While he was at it, Peter Carlsen happened past. Though we are separated by nearly a kilometer, he is my nearest neighbor to the south. He and the grocer together pushed the vehicle out of the ditch while I tripped alongside and steered. After-wards I asked them both in for coffee and we sat at my tiny blue table in the kitchen, there was hardly room for us. I told Peter Carlsen what a pleasure it is to have Carl come to visit.

It was a pleasure for him too, he said. Rosenstand is really rather bustling and unsettled in nature.

What am I to do, with no one to look after and everything taken care of? Am I to be an outcast? Is that now to be my obligation, as it is my obligation to mourn? If so, it would perhaps be easier for me to understand. No matter. I do not constantly mourn.

Bicycling is out of the question as long as there is snow. I have started going for walks again.

The sound of a beck in February is a rich sound indeed. There is the water and the glittering ice. The water is almost black at this time of year, as black as the bed it runs upon.

I am looking forward to seeing what will apear when spring comes. I have already found two great Christmas roses on the south side of the house, and in the windbreak, where the snow is not quite as thick, there are snowdrops and eranthis. In the thousands.

Peter Carlsen thought the house had been done so nicely. He said so as he left. He leaned forward slightly, and because

I thought he was going to shake hands I put out my hand. Instead, he placed a little figurine of a woman in my palm. He had made it himself at his kitchen table, from some leftover putty he had picked up and absently begun to shape. "For you, Fru Bagge," he said. We did not look at each other. There was a warmth from him.

It was the same warmth as then. I could feel it despite our standing apart. How peculiar that it should happen here in the hall after so many years, with the grocer on his knees at the living-room stove, rattling the vents. Yet the feeling is not of mutual joy, but more of hope yet to be hoped, and that is enough to unsettle me. For was that warmth in fact my own? Did I wish to burn it up and reduce it to ashes? Closing the door after him, I glimpsed myself in the mirror, and there I stood with blushing cheeks.

I have put his little figurine on top of the grandfather clock in the hall. No visitor will see it there. But I will see it. The very moment after I had put it down, Rosenstand came out into the hall. "There we are," he said. "It should give you no bother the rest of the day. I can't promise it'll stay that way, mind you."

February 6

I am deflated. I sit in a chair in the living room and do nothing, immersed in the thought of Peter Carlsen being so acquainted with women as to be able to shape one with his hands. Vigand too was acquainted with women, though only as a physician. One senses in a man how much or how little he cares for the woman. It has been a sport for me all these years, and has kept me going, because I always thought it to be hidden away in Vigand, and that all I had to do was bring it out. I have only myself to thank, since he did nothing to encourage me. Occasionally, my will can be quite ruthless, and for long periods it has made me unhappy.

Not that I think he cared more for men. People interested him perhaps only by virtue of their stupidity. Often I have sat and watched him in company and seen how his showing an interest in people would encourage them to be talkative, oblivious to the fact that he did so only so that he might afterwards delight in their shortcomings. He observed people with the cold detachment of a scientist. One evening, when we were still living in Give, a car came up to the house, and Clemmens Mathiesen from Riis got out and knocked on the door. He had come with a message from his neighbor, it was urgent, the man's false teeth were stuck in his throat. It was a Thursday, and Vigand had been looking forward to the evening, he had invited three others to the house for a game of Ombre, and he replied that either the man would be dead by the time they got there, or else the dentures would have dislodged and come up of their own accord, and as such the matter was simply not worth his while. Nevertheless, Mathiesen managed to convince him, and when they reached the farm they found the neighbour sitting on a chair with the dentures in his hand. "See for yourself, Mathiesen," said Vigand, "What did I tell you." I have the story not from Vigand, but from gossip in the town, though I have no reason to doubt it on that account. He could be rude. Once, he had arranged with the carrier man from Give to be driven, and when the driver came and asked where they were going, Vigand replied: "To hell, for all I care." I heard it myself from the step.

I think of such episodes when former bitterness returns. It can go deeper still, to something hard and strong as salt, though quite as bitter.

Hilda squeezed my hands so hearteningly. "A *lady*," she said. But Vigand, who sees through everything, takes a different view. "A one-eyed woman in the country of the blind, more like it," he says. "How about putting your money to better use?"

"What would you suggest?" I ask, with genuine interest. But Vigand has never been keen on providing answers, nor, for that matter, on asking questions.

He knows me so well. He knows, without ever having broached the subject, that my path has been decided by nothing else but chance, and that my inclinations have been towards, if not another, for I cannot be quite as categorical as that, then at least in some other direction. He considered me uneducated. He is right. He considered me primitive too, at the mercy of my emotions. In all the years we were married, I endeavored to speak in such a way that he would not think me stupid. Now I can be as stupid as I like. I bury my face in my hands.

How forceful this bitterness, even though I now have everything the way I want. Pause for thought indeed.

I have lit the lamp, but not even that helps.

February 8

Several mornings of frosty mist. This morning the temperature was twelve degrees below freezing, the lowest all winter. The rime clung to the trees long after the sun came out. The garden is dotted with the tracks of the hare, it looks like a whole drove was here. The birds in the tree say nothing, there is barely a movement anywhere.

I went for a walk. I must find new walks now. I am keeping a low profile at the moment. I went in the southerly direction, past Hedebjerg Farm. Its avenue of trees was white, wrapped up in the frost. It was a quiet morning, but this afternoon there have been visitors. Pastor Grell and his wife came to see the house, and Rosenstand was here too. I did not offer him coffee today. After he had gone, Carl came. He had brought seeds with him, in envelopes with the seed type written on each. Poppy, marigold, runner bean, sweet pea, curly kale.

"You brought me seeds?" I asked in mild surprise.

"No, they're from my father," he said.

Immediately, I recognized the handwriting.

He said the curly kale should be pre-sprouted without

delay. We found some old pots stacked up in a box on top of a shelf in the outhouse. I wondered about the soil, it was frozen. "We'll use some compost," he said. He knew where the heap was at the bottom of the garden and filled up a bucket for me. We put it in the cellar where it will stay warm.

And the sun is high. It is only two o'clock.

February 9

Today is also cold. This morning the thermometer said minus nine, and the smoke rises straight in the air. It is transparent, a mere shimmer above the roof. There is not a breath of wind.

On such a crisp and frosty day, Carl and Dagmar stood as small children in the yard in front of the farmhouse and heard the hospital wagon come from Give to collect their mother, who lay dying from the Spanish flu. They could hear the horses for a whole hour, far away on the other side of Dørken, he told me yesterday. He was quite matter-of-fact about it, as is his habit.

"Oh, Carl," I said.

"Yes," he said.

He had photographs with him. Undoubtedly for my pleasure, there were a couple from the living room in the doctor's residence. I saw the gramophone, and my own astonished face like a spirit's, staring out from the sofa.

I think I shall sing for a while.

Yes.

I met Peter Carlsen at Hansen's grocery shop one Saturday afternoon a fortnight after I had been out at Hedebjerg Farm asking for him. I was on my way out, he on his way in.

"Did you get my message?" I asked.

"No," he said.

"I spoke to your mother and Henriette."

"I didn't know."

"They must have forgotten," I said.

"They don't usually," he said.

We lowered our voices. Not that there was any need, no one could hear us, we were standing on the step. But the moment I saw him, my very being descended into a more ponderous tenor. To speak so solemnly and so softly, as if oblivious to the greater forces at play. Even my legs felt heavy.

"Is Bernhard with you?" I asked.

"He's waiting in the cart. He prefers it that way. You can come and say hello to him."

He took my basket out of my hand. We patted Bernhard and made such a fuss of him I can hardly imagine he had ever been the object of such attention before. Nor had I ever felt such warmth in my presence, but I recognized it immediately. I told him about my plans to make a garden for the children, with trees and bushes for shelter.

That same evening he came walking over the meadow. He wanted us to consider the matter before the sun went down.

I suggested lilac and jasmine, fruit trees and a kitchen garden. He said we should begin with several rows of white spruce against the wind.

"How long will it take?" I asked.

"A long time," he replied.

As dusk came, we went for a walk in the direction of Hedebjerg Farm to see a newborn calf. We walked over the fields and saw no one. The grass was fragrant, the heather was fragrant. We stood and watched the calf and its mother until it was almost dark. Some distance away the lamps were lit on the farm, and I turned towards him and for some reason whispered rather than saying the words out loud: "Would you care for a cup of coffee?"

"Yes," he whispered back.

We walked back to the school. We saw no one.

Thoughts are superfluous. For of all the things that may be imagined or said, nothing bears comparison to being held in his embrace, when that happened. Of all the things my hands and body have done, this is what they remember best, and I do not wish to forget it.

~

I will write about today. What has happened? Various visitors, much coffee drinking. Reading. I have joined Fru Grell's reading group and we have been given homework. We are to read *Birds Around the Light* by Jacob Paludan and have had some difficulty getting hold of it. The library in Give have not yet received a copy, and so we have been compelled to purchase our own and must make do with taking turns. It is quite an extravagance, and Fru Grell was not pleased with the solution at all, but she has been so buoyant at the thought of our keeping abreast of contemporary works. I felt quite sorry for her when complaints were murmured. After lunch a walk up the hill in the direction of Hedebjerg Farm. I turned back before I got to the top. It was so windy I had to keep my hand on my hat the whole time. With the wind the temperature is rising and is now above freezing. Hour by hour, the snow in the garden has sunk. I took some snowdrops in and arranged them in a glass.

Just before, as I was lining the shelves in the scullery, a

thought occurred to me that I shall put here as a question and answer: What is community? It is work and love. But it is also to stand outside. Someone must point to what it is. Someone has to know.

I find it to be rather a comfort.

February 12

Why should I torment myself?

For no reason, just as I have no reason to arrange my breakfast so nicely with the starched napkin on the tray that I carry over to the sofa by the window. The trees are swaying, and the garden suddenly looks grubby. It is a dismal day. Two degrees above freezing. When I came into the living room a short time ago, I noticed a hare gnawing at one of the fruit trees. It was standing on its hind legs, gripping the trunk with its front paws. I opened a window and shouted at it. It was so indifferent it hardly twitched a whisker. I had to put my boots on and go out to chase it away.

~

I stood in his arms in the kitchen, and his chest was against my chest, his arms were around me, and I was filled by a single sentence: "For now is a new time." It was not a thought, but a fullness that manifested itself in the words. He lowered his lips to my ear and his voice was a measured whisper: "I am not free."

I drew myself up and sank down at once, and he gripped me even tighter.

"Then you must choose," I said and pulled away. I ran into the living room, and he ran after me. I ran into the schoolroom and stood in front of the glass-fronted cupboard, and he came after me.

"We must talk," he said.

"No, you must go," I said.

"Do you really want me to go?" he said, and tears welled in his eyes.

"Yes."

"If only this had happened three weeks ago – a fortnight ago."

"I don't want to hear about it," I said.

"I didn't think you cared for me."

"Please, no excuses."

"I only wanted to be with you."

"Then break off your engagement."

There was a pause.

"Is it your cousin?"

"She and I have known each other since we were little."

"I'm sure she'll make a good wife on a farm like yours."

"How did you know?" he asked, surprised.

And before I answered he buried his face in the hollow of my shoulder, and I curled my arm around his neck, and my other arm around his back, and both of us wept.

~

As I sat at the table there was a knock on the door. It was almost twelve o'clock and I felt no inclination to see who it was. But it turned out to be none other than Peder Møllergaard. He stood leaning on his walking stick on the step. He had walked from Lunds Farm into the town and had decided to stop by on his way back. He declined coffee and preferred not to sit. He glanced around the living room and must surely have noticed the remains of my breakfast. "Bright and unpretentious," he said appreciatively. I coaxed him into sitting down despite his reluctance. He asked if I was happy with the house.

"For we are indeed happy that you chose to stay, Fru Bagge."

I have no idea what would make him say such a thing.

He told me that the parish book collection, housed at the Young Men's and Women's Christian Association, is at present without supervision, and asked if the position could interest me.

"I don't think there's much of a salary," he said, with his back half turned.

I made no comment.

"It would please me," he said, "if you would take it on."

I have written him a few lines and dropped the envelope through the letter box at the savings bank. The bells were ringing for afternoon service. I went in and listened to that peculiar verse about the seed falling in the stony places and on the good ground. I have always found it odd, since it seems to me to be one of the easiest to understand. And yet the disciples ask what it means, and Jesus becomes so impatient when prompted to explain it to them that his explanation ends up in the most impenetrable riddles, those unknowing of the kingdom of heaven are to be addressed in parables, he says, so "that seeing they may see, and not perceive; and hearing they may hear, and not grasp; lest at any time they should be converted, and their sins should be forgiven them." But why should they be kept from forgiveness?

We sang "Come, Rain from the Heavens."

Vigand would say I was a fool.

Peter Carlsen was there with Dagmar, Inge, and Carl. All four in heavy overcoats. When I thanked him for the seeds, he said there were more where they came from. I walked home, and am now exhausted.

February 13

The wind has raged without pause for thirty hours, and I am queasy and out of sorts. I went out along the road with both hands on my hat and was almost tossed into the ditch. No visitors today, not even Rosenstand. I have a small dried sausage for my dinner, but the wind has taken away my appetite. This afternoon I thought of going to see Hilda, but would she care for a visit? I am sure she would be more flustered than glad. Often, when one is most in need of company, one hesitates at the thought of appearing to be in straits. Imagine, if one were unable to let go again.

I am waiting for Vigand to make himself known. Where are you, Vigand? Say something. Box my ears!

The lawn is strewn with fallen branches, a rather large one and a lot of smaller ones. The wind huffs and puffs at the house, the electricity went out quite some time ago. Now, as darkness comes, I light the lamp. I place it in the window. The panes rattle, the flame flickers.

February 14

When Peter Carlsen married Henriette it happened so quickly that people in the town said there was a reason. I am sure
there was, but not the one they meant. It was a Saturday in
spring. I had my singing duties to fulfill and was standing in
the choir loft. There was a drizzle in the air, spring rain. I sang
facing sideways and without looking down, for I imagined he
felt the same as I did, and I did not wish to embarrass him
with my own embarrassment and grief. My voice was pure
and clear in those days, unerring. But when I got home I
went into the kitchen, drew out a chair, flopped forward on
the table, and fell asleep. I was wakened by a hand stroking
my hair.

It was a hand unaccustomed to caressing. It was fearful,
afraid of causing me harm. I thought, has all the badness
gone away? I sat up and turned my head, then leapt to my
feet at once, because the hand caressing me belonged to
Jens Kristian Andersen. Petting-Jens. I got up so quickly the
blood rushed to my head and I fainted.

I came round to find his beard against my brow. I had no sense of what was going on, and no realization that it was Jens Kristian. I heard a groan, and something being dragged over the floor. Later, I understood it to be my own feet, my heels were rubbed white by their passage across the floorboards. He freed an arm so as to open the door of the chamber and laid me down on the bed. He was all in a tizzy, made to loosen my dress, but decided against it, went to fetch some water and then spilled it on top of me, causing me to sit up with a jolt; he pressed me down again and dried me with a pillow, and urged: "Lie still, lie still." I could not have found a clumsier attendant. He stayed at my side in the chamber, seated on a chair. I was ill at ease with the situation and pretended to sleep. Whenever I peeped he was still there. Sometimes he was staring out the window. Sometimes he was staring at me. I was so exhausted that I did not have the strength to ask him to leave.

And now Hilda, who came here this morning, tells me he died in the storm that blew across the land the day before yesterday. His mother's house fell down on top of him, and hours later he expired at the hospital in Give. The funeral has been arranged for the day after tomorrow. No doubt there will be many in attendance, if only because he was his mother's son. However, the circumstances of his death will also surely swell the numbers.

I wonder if he ever received any of Vigand's clothes? A comfort to think that he wouldn't have cared two hoots.

One cannot do without a single soul. And yet it is not true. Now and again, a rage flares into my throat.

VB

VB

VB

He knew I was angling for a tender word that I might go on. A whole life together had taught him as much.

But if you only knew, Vigand, that I walk the floors of my nice new home and spit the words out loud: You Bloody Bastard. What would you say then?

Promptly comes the answer: "Frankly, you can do as you want."

His voice is not arrogant, but tired.

He is dead. He has reason to be tired.

It comes over me in fits that rattle my frame. I am sitting on the sofa with the newspaper. It is afternoon, and the sun has come out. Its light is feeble and grey. Hares in the garden.

February 18

The sun has been out for several days, and in the night the temperature has dropped to fifteen below. I was at the churchyard yesterday, the headstone has arrived and I wanted to go and see it. For some reason, the mason has carved the name in the middle, as if the stone were for him only. I asked for the name and title to be prominent, but not for that. And yet I must say that a relief came over me, and I am rather uplifted still, not at the thought of escaping death – no one could be that silly – but at not having to be put there beside him. It is only a thought. I will be put beside him.

~

I went outside and tidied the garden after the storm. One of the branches that had fallen down was so big I had to saw it up just to shift it. It was quite a job, the saw was too small. I think I would like a pet to keep. A dog or a cat, perhaps also some hens for the hen-house, something to attach me to the place. For dinner I made stuffed cabbage leaves. I played

Patience at the table in the living room, relieved that not a soul had come to see me all day.

There is something wrong. I have moved away from others. Society does not exist here where I am. Which is how things become heedless.

February 25

After a period of fatigue and listlessness so compelling that I would not go to the door when anyone knocked, I lay in my bed this morning and thought of how little it mattered whether I got up or not. If I wanted, I could stay there all day. It was lovely to be in bed. I had drawn up the blind and the air was clear. The light is returning in the mornings.

I thought of Vigand, and the fact that we got married, and I found it singular indeed. We hardly knew each other. I had seen him twice when he proposed. Thrice, if his talk on kitchen hygiene is to be included.

The second time was when the children received their smallpox vaccinations. Vigand came at the last minute. I was commandeered to help. One by one, they stepped up to the desk, and I held their hands while he disinfected the skin on their upper arms. A brisk wipe with a swab of cotton wool. "Go home and tell your mother to give you a bath," he instructed many. "Now you'll feel a little jab. Nothing to cry about. There, all finished. Not too bad, was it? And you don't like chocolate, do you?"

"Yes."

"You don't say. Lucky for you, I've brought some with me."

They were as quiet as mice. For some of them it was probably the first time in their lives they had been given a whole piece of chocolate wrapped up in silver paper, all for themselves. They must have been hoping there was enough to go round.

When he was done he packed his bag, but instead of leaving he asked if we would mind if he sat at the back of the class and listened. He promised not to cause trouble. The children stared at him gravely, which could seem rude to anyone unfamiliar with them, but they were oblivious to the notion that others could find them interesting. Something that by no means exclusively applies to children.

We were having arithmetic and had got as far as to the multiplication tables from 2 to 10, which we sat and chanted. We loved to chant. Vigand raised a finger in the air. "Can I ask a question?"

I nodded.

"Does anyone here know what naught plus naught plus naught plus naught plus naught is?" he asked. Silence descended, no one dared say a word; the older ones, who would have known, said nothing either. Eventually, little Ludvig Ludvigsen ventured in a trembling voice: "Five?"

After I had said goodbye to the children I thought he would be on his way. But he was still standing there in the schoolroom when I came back in, and I asked if I could offer him anything. "A cup of coffee," he said.

I had to go and light the stove and was afraid he would tire of waiting. When I came back with a tray he was looking in one of the school books he had taken from the glass-fronted cupboard and seemed to be enjoying it. "Go to the ant and be wise," he read out loud in a measured voice. "What splen-did nonsense."

He was satisfied with the school, particularly the light that came into the room, the high ceiling, and the ventilation panes in the great windows. I remember him asking about the drinking water and where the washrooms were situated. "A far cry from Kokborg School," he said. "They shit and drink in the same place there."

We drank our coffee. "You're not as spry as last time I saw you," he said, and narrowed an eye. "You're looking a bit peaky. And you've lost weight. Can you not keep your food down?"

The moment he mentioned it, I felt straight away that I

had to be sick. I managed to get to the hall, where I grabbed the floor bucket and kicked open the door of my rooms.

When I came back, he said: "Let me have a look at you."

"Nothing to worry about," he said after a minute. "You're not dying."

He had very blue eyes, Vigand. They gleamed.

The most puzzling thing to have occurred in my fifty-year life is that he returned two days later. He came striding up Nørregade in a grey suit and hat, and without his doctor's bag. He had sent the driver to the inn. He wondered if he could come in, and asked whether or not I was aware that my comings and goings were being observed and that while Nørregade at that moment seemed deserted it would soon be common knowledge that he had come to visit. "We can go for a walk if you want," he said. "Not that it would alter anything."

We made an arc around the town and strolled out towards Hastrup.

He said: "We might as well be married right away, now that we've given them something to talk about." And then he took my hand. "You'll be a good wife," he added, as though it were a consolation. Vigand had what they call pudgy fingers. It was odd for such a slender man. They were very thick lower down and tapered thinner at the tips. It was a problem with regard to the wedding ring, he had difficulty finding one that would stay on, and it was out of the question for him to wear it when he was working. Imagine if he were to lose it inside someone. He kept it in a Petri dish in his desk during the daytime, and would put it on when his work was done. Once, it fell off when he was fetching peat from the cellar, and we were unable to find it anywhere. I searched for days, while Vigand retreated into displeasure. It turned up in the garden underneath the dripping eaves when the snow melted in the spring. It was the housemaid who found it, she came in and held it up in triumph. I put it on his breakfast plate and said nothing, looking forward to seeing his face when he came down and found it there. But all he did was put it on, unfold the newspaper, and begin to read.

Vigand preferred a civil marriage, but it was such a nuisance to arrange that we were married in the church at Give instead. We made it a quiet affair, not even Agnete or my parents were there. Vigand procured a bridal bouquet, and when it withered he threw it out.

We never spoke of what prompted us to marry. There

was a grace about him. Without wishing for even the smallest word of gratitude, he assumed to have saved me. He must have allowed for another man's child being part of the bargain, but even when it turned out there was none, he refrained from comment. I loved him for it, and yet it has often driven me mad with speculation. Why did he take me? Was he really just being chivalrous? Throughout our entire marriage, I have by turns considered either that there was no reason at all, or that there was a reason, which I would surely find, if only I looked hard enough.

I begged him that we might have children.

"You can't have children, as you well know," he said.

It was the worst of anything that was said between us. It left a stain on my soul that cannot be erased. I had hoped that Vigand would remove it.

I had hoped for a caress.

The tantrums I have thrown.

April 19 1929

I find much pleasure in the hens. When I have been down to open the hatch in the mornings, they dash to the fence and watch me wistfully as I go back to the house. After lunch I let them out of the run, and shortly afterwards they are clucking and scraping all over the garden, except the kitchen garden, which Carl has fenced off. Most have particular friends whose company they prefer. One encounters them unexpectedly in some snug little hiding place or enjoying a dust-bath down by the pond. They love the spring and sunshine. They tidy their feathers as if they were shaking sand from a towel, settle themselves more comfortably and cluck softly to each other. But there are outcasts too. Hilda refers to one as the Brave One, because it seems always to be harried by the others, and whenever she finds the chance she will pick it up in her arms and make a fuss of it, to spite the others and make them envious. In the summer, when the French doors were left open, they would often venture into the dining room to see me. They were the politest of visitors, calling out to ask if they were welcome, and whenever I appeared too abruptly from another room they would scatter and fall over themselves in a rush to be gone.

Last week, I took the car up to Hedebjerg Farm to ask Inge and Dagmar if they would care for a drive. I have been putting it off for months, telling myself that I ought to take them on a proper trip, for instance to Fakkegrav, where they could visit the sea and have tea at the hotel there. But it seemed so insurmountable. Instead, we took a little jaunt out to Hastrup Pond and visited the mill, where we bought cordial that we drank while sitting on a bench as the wheel turned and turned at our rear. Afterwards we drove home to Rose Cottage. Dagmar and Inge sat out in the garden, and I went down to the hen-house and scooped the newly hatched chicks up into a shallow cardboard box. It had given me the whole idea for our trip that day. Indeed, it was to be the high-light. I was so looking forward to showing Inge the chicks that it would be untrue to claim that my motives were entirely unselfish. Cautiously, I placed the box in her lap. Dagmar guided her hand towards them, and Inge's face instantly lit up in a smile. She felt them with her hands, each and every one. Oh, their little black eyes, and oh, their little cheeps and chirps. It was such a lovely day. I lifted one out of the box and placed it in her hand, and Inge lowered her other hand carefully on top of it like a lid and uttered some quick and whispered sounds. Dagmar leaned over her shoulder and put her cheek to hers, and she too picked a chick up in her hand. Transports of delight. Such a day we had.

Why do I think of it now? Because Hilda and I had to slaughter three hens today. For some time now they have produced eggs with double yolks. Eggs that have been much too big, with far too much calcium in the shell. And I had determined with certainty which of them it was, having hovered about the nesting boxes and observed their comings and goings. But I had been unable to prevail on myself to do the necessary. This morning when I let them out, one of them was trailing its insides behind it, and the others were giving it a hard time. That settled the matter, and we chopped the heads off the other two as well. Hilda and I had a jolly afternoon. We carried a garden table into the yard, where the fowl were plucked and prepared. Hilda is so very clever with her hands, and did such a fine job. Drawing geese is the best, she tells me, hens the next best. I gave her two to take home with her and kept one for myself. I shall make broth tomorrow.

I have been at the book collection this evening, as on every other during the week, apart from Tuesday, when we are closed. Opening time is from five until nine. In addition, we are open on Saturday afternoons between two and five.

The days spent at home at Rose Cottage are delightful, but when evening comes I prefer to be at the books. Now it is properly the spring, not only when the sun shines, but also when the afternoons draw to a close and twilight falls. The boys play marbles on the footpath to the church, and the further away from winter we get, the more intricate and wide-reaching their games become. They have told me there can be several hundred marbles involved at a time. Like their fathers before them, they collect the lead seals from the grocer Hansen's sacks of field seed and take them to Martin Dreyer, who owns the necessary forceps, and have their marbles made by him. On such an evening, when a blackbird sings from the roof of the inn, and another replies from the grocer Rosenstand's roof, one may think nothing to be lovelier than a little town with its high street and shops, its children and all the homes whose lamps are lit in the windows, for outside the town there is only the very dark land.

Our book collection is not fine by any stretch of the imagination. It is housed in a space for which no other use could be found. I have seen pictures of high-ceilinged library rooms with reading desks and a dimness illuminated by green reading lamps, made for the very purpose of absorption. I should very much like the people of Thyregod to see such a room. When I first took up the position, Peder Møllergaard impressed upon me that no means were available to squander, but he might just as well have saved his breath. One hardly needed to examine the accounts to understand that barely a krone had been spent in years, and that the collection had in recent decades for the most part been extended only by gifts from people who could not bring themselves to throw out a volume. Much as I left Vigand's books behind for the new physician, so people have deposited their rubbish here. The greatest culprits have been the various pastors, betrayed by their names that are written inside. Pastor Grell, too, has divested himself of much godly reading material. I imagine these bequeathments to be the result of spring cleaning. In short, the junk that has acccumulated here can hardly be estimated. Not to mention the dirt. Dusty would be a sorely inadequate characterization of the place when I first started, and many of the books were so filthy one could scrape the grime from their covers with a knife. I have burned many volumes in the stove because of the health hazard alone. The lot has been cleaned: shelves and books, ceiling, walls, and floor. Before going home at night, I mop the floor, but even airing the room once a day can work wonders.

I have been greatly helped by consulting *The Library Journal* and Vejle Central Library, which I have visited on several occasions and whose staff have provided me with instruction and lent me manuals on the correct procedures for cataloguing and lending, as well as other materials concerning a library's day-to-day running. They even sent out a traveling librarian, who helped me to set out the books according to the decimal system and to divide up the fiction, so that there are now separate shelves for children's books, poetry, and drama, and moreover for handbooks and works of reference that may only be consulted on the premises.

It awakened a certain interest in our otherwise so unheeded collection that I began to clear out and catalogue, and even be open at times when people were able to come. Peder Møllergaard also took an interest in the matter. When I asked the parish council for money for filing boxes and registers, he commissioned Haagensen the cabinet maker to construct a desk of oak with drawers and cupboards and two inbuilt filing boxes, and besides that two large reading tables, one with partitions at each end and side, allowing four people to sit and read and yet remain undisturbed by one another, and when the desk and the tables had been installed I invited the parish council and the members of the Civic and Tradesmen's Association to come and see the place, and demonstrated the principles of book shelving, the filing cards and the new system of borrowers' cards and book slips that I had acquired from the library in Vejle. I also showed them the register of books, in which not a single new purchase had been entered since 1921. They wandered about and looked at the half-empty shelves. I didn't tell them how much I had incinerated or thrown out. My feeling was that they would be better convinced by lack of quantity than by lack of quality, and that they would come to doubt my judgement if I told them about the many volumes I had eliminated.

The result of their visit is that I have been given a sum of money by the parish council and the Civic and Tradesmen's Association, to be spent on new books. They would like a modern collection that is in keeping with the times. They asked if I was able to bind the books myself so that we might save the expense of a professional. I am able, albeit with difficulty. Agnete learned how to do it when she was a young woman, and I watched her. That forgotten knowledge comes back to me in drips. I began by repairing the oldest and tattiest volumes, and gradually I have ventured into new bindings from scratch. I stand at home in the scullery of Rose Cottage with such work.

Last spring the garden was left to itself. Carl tells me it is time now to remedy the matter, and he says he will help me. He came yesterday and dug up the kitchen garden, and the weather was so warm we could sit with our coffee in the nook by the wash-house and the peat-house. The hens were out enjoying themselves in the sunshine. I had baked some shortbread.

As we sat there, Carl said he would like to live here at Rose Cottage with Dagmar and Inge after his father dies.

"What would you do with the place?" I asked.

"Keep bees," he answered.

"Is it a good place for bees?"

"Yes."

"Your father's not ill, is he?" I asked after a pause.

"I don't think so," he replied deliberately, as if he were not quite sure. But then one never can be sure.

May 2

The grocer Rosenstand is to be married. The town has been a babble of chatter for weeks, and now it has been announced, the date fixed for June 1. He is so kind towards me that I think he must feel guilty. There is so much talk of it. It is not common to marry at such an advanced age. Next year he will be sixty, and Kirsten Vinge, his wife-to-be, is soon approaching fifty. She is the daughter of the former bailiff from Vester, but although she is fine and dainty in appearance, no one had ever imagined she would be married, for she is lame and has always lived on her own in a little house by the road between Thyregod and Vester. Ever since she was quite young, she has made her living as a seamstress. I once had a pair of dresses made by her. Her living room was so bare, and a sheet of loose linoleum covered the floor. It was an oddly cold and dismal home. In the middle of the room was her sewing machine, and there was hardly a piece of furniture besides. It was indeed a trial to be fitted by her, for she is so very exacting and takes an age in everything she does. One stands until racked with fatigue, with pins pricking one's skin, while she crawls about the floor adjusting her work with cold, thin hands. But Rosenstand earns more than enough to keep them both, and Hilda says she has already given up her sewing. They seem to be happy, and quite indifferent to the gossip they must surely be aware has been sweeping through the town.

I have only now dug up the fruit trees that were gnawed away by the hares last winter and put them on the waste pile. Again, Carl was here to help me. He came with a greeting from his father who said there were some new fruit trees for me at Hedebjerg if I wished for some, and so I drove up there this afternoon. He had put aside six in all: two Victoria plum, Guldborg and Filippa apple, Grise-Bonne and August pear. There was not enough room in the car, so he drove them home for me, and planted them too. The only thing I had to do was hold them straight. While he was fetching more water, the thatcher came driving along the road, and when he saw me standing beside one of the small trees he shouted over the hedge: "*Those wud'nae bae love apples?*"

"What was he wanting?" Peter asked when he came back.

"I didn't quite catch," I said.

We had coffee in the nook, and I told him that I had taken

out subscriptions on the *Folk High School Journal* and *Danish Horizon* for the book collection.

When I was at Hedebjerg this afternoon, Inge came out through the French doors with a pair of scissors in her hand and walked through the garden so proudly upright and with such purpose in her step that anyone, I am certain, would have thought she could see. She bent down and cut a handful of chives, before going back up the path and into the house.

"Such marvelous daughters you have," I said to Peter.

"Good daughters, yes," he replied, and I was at a loss as to whether he was correcting me or merely adding something else. Whatever it was, I think it was just right.

We had such fun planting the trees, not that I can recall what we talked about. But the mood was lighthearted, the work unfussed, and we laughed. It felt almost as if we were young again. Yet thinking back now, I cannot recall us ever having fun when we were young. In those days, there was a solemn restraint between us that kept us apart, because something blind and serious was tunnelling forth. And of course it did become serious, and blind in the sense that it was unattainable.

In all the years that have passed, I have pictured him the way he looked as he came walking over the meadow that evening to teach me how to grow a garden. It had just rained and he was wet across the shoulders, and I knew he would be fragrant with the smell of grass and livestock. He told me a cow had just calved, and asked me if I would like to see the calf. So we walked through the gloaming and came to the calf, that was sucking its mother's milk. We were serious in those days. Tremulous.

May 17

On such an evening in May, when a pale blush falls into the room, the book collection can be rather a delightful place. People are quiet in here, save for a hushed murmur at the children's shelf. Yesterday evening, which was Saturday, the chatterbox was Janus Vestergaard's eldest son, who has already found an interest in girls, and they in him. He sat with two, slightly older than himself, and entertained them with a stack of books in his lap. The borrowers came and went all evening, and now and again I tidied up. I know most of them by sight, but at the reading table there was a man I was unable to recall having seen before. Peter Carlsen sat immersed in a copy of *Danish Horizon* for more than an hour at the same table. I have put summer curtains up and had the collection's rules and regulations framed, and there are new pictures on the walls now: an ordnance survey map of Vejle's western tracts from 1919 and a print showing the battle of Sankelmark, where Aksel Nielsen of Hindskov, who is long since dead, was wounded in the hip. When I first came here, people still told stories about 1864 on Saturday evenings when they got together at Hansen's grocery. Everyone knew what Aksel Nielsen and apparently several others from the district had been through, and yet none of it was ever talked about. The stories they told were funny and down-to-earth, and concerned only with the trivial things. Jens Thiis and his brothers could not be chased to bed and would sit, wilting and pale with fatigue, waiting for the exciting parts that never came.

As closing time approached, most of the borrowers had gone home and I went about making sure the books were in order on the shelves. I turned the lamp off on the desk and began to turn off the other lights too as a sign that we were closing. The children left, and Peter Carlsen came and said goodbye, but the man from before was still there at the reading table.

"We're closing now," I said.

"Lilly," he said.

I stopped in my tracks. He got to his feet. He was a big man. I had no idea who he might be. I stood and looked at him, and then his name popped out of my mouth.

"Erland," I blurted. "What are you doing here?"

And we both began to laugh.

"Have you eaten?" he asked.

"Not really," I said. "Have you?"

"Not really."

"We can't go to the inn here," I said. "They'll think we're getting married, or worse."

"How about the hotel in Give?" he suggested.

It turned out that he had taken a room there. He had come to Thyregod on the train, and so we agreed to take the car. Unsurprisingly, we were seen on our way to Rose Cottage to pick it up, so we might just as well have gone to the inn, but I gave not a thought to the matter; I was so excited that he had come.

By the time we came to the high street in Give, I had returned so much to my senses as to become embarrased at the thought of sitting in the sight of the dear Fru Lorentzen, but the fact was that we would be lucky if we could get anything at all to eat at that time of the evening. The kitchen was indeed closed, and though it was not without a sigh, she took pity on us and sent the waitresses in with vegetable broth and cold meat with bread and mustard to go with it, and then they came with beer too. Apart from ourselves, only a few other diners remained in the room. We sat by the French doors, behind the flower arrangement. We were both so happy and surprised to see each other. I asked him what on earth had brought him here, and he told me he had heard about me from Ervin and his wife, and that he had felt the urge to come and see me, now that he knew where I lived. We went our separate ways when we were still young, and because so much time has elapsed what lies in between can hardly be passed over. But in those days I looked at him differently and always thought he wore his clothes as if somehow he were rather helplessly naked. His waistcoat would be buttoned too high, and his jacket was far too tight, his movements in it awkward and unaccustomed, giving the impression that he was not yet properly a man, though he was big and muscular even then. And he sang so loudly and out of tune that I preferred to shuffle away from him, though no distance was ever sufficient for it not to ruin one's concentration, and his laughter was so boisterous as to be nearly a roar. And all this I remembered with astonishment, for the recollection was no longer real, but a recollection of a recollection, or an image of an image of an image. And yet that is not true, because the recollection of these helplessly human qualities, which I had not appreciated at the time, prompted me then to lean forward towards him, and I cannot say anything but that I was glad.

Indeed.

Erland has in many ways led a disheartened life, though he now runs a free school up by the Limfjord. He told me about his compelling infatuation for his young student at Ubberup, which had taken him years to get over, despite his having known all along that it was wrong, in the sense of being destructive to all parties, to himself, to her, to his wife, and most of all to his children, he said, and then he looked down at his plate and fell silent.

"Do you see them sometimes?" I asked.

"No," he said.

In the continuing silence, something happened that was not at all like a house abruptly settling or something sinking inside my chest, but a warmth unfolded and spread. I know now that it was tenderness. I did nothing, but I could have taken his hand without shame, because I saw his nature and understood it, it was familiar to me, and at the same time I knew that the same held for my part, and that he, as he sat there, was quite as familiar with me and knew that I too was helplessly human, and I knew that he would never wish for it to be any different.

Forgive them, for they know only what they do, as he considered Jesus ought to have said.

We parted in the hall. He took my hand and I wriggled my fingers into the warm cup of his palm.

I went out and started the car, and was home shortly after midnight. I lay in my bed for seven hours, but I did not sleep.

May 22

I told Hilda that I have met an old student friend who runs a free school in Himmerland, and she looked at me with wide eyes. All at once, they filled with tears. I think she found the news so singular that there was nothing else she could do but cry. I said nothing of the circumstances of my meeting this old friend, but she understood immediately, and her question, albeit unuttered, was this: "An old woman like you? Are you a stranger after all?"

What am I to say? Yes, I am a stranger, though oddly enough I am not unprepared. My heart runs on ahead of me. And I, I run after my heart. I cannot be without it.

Erland is in Viborg to give a talk and has taken the car. We had not anticipated that the weather would take such a turn. Snow on the first of November. It is not snowing much. The thermometer says zero degrees.

We talked about Hallow-Eve in school today, and the children made lanterns. In Thyregod we cut faces in the turnips, the eerier the better, but the sugar beet they use here make a serene and blushing glow that is so very good for lanterns. They cut out suns and stars and moons, and strung their lanterns up among the trees at the pond.

Just before, as I passed the French doors, I discovered they have been into our garden too. Lanterns in the trees, and one on the compost heap. Wherever I look, to the garden or to the road, there are lanterns. There is even one in the pear tree at the side of the house. Erland will be tickled when he comes home.

The radio says the snow is from the south and that there is more to come.

I have thought much about my lonely time, which has

become so distant and yet may suddenly well inside me and feel exactly as before, if ever I happen to be alone for an afternoon and evening. The merest reminder of that time is more than sufficient. It is not a recollection of a recollection, or an image of an image. Never again do I wish to be alone, and what I mean is that I never again wish to be without Erland. No love is ever without grief. I must confess that when I was married to Vigand I often thought, when he was out in the car on such a night, that if he were to have an accident I would manage. And more so, that I would finally be myself alone. But in Erland's case I worry. I have no desires to be myself alone.

He must soon be here.

I was thinking about how I arrived here. Like a twig suddenly dislodged from the bank of a stream, then carried along by a racing current. That helpless sense of motion. "I couldn't stop myself from writing to you," he said.

"I'm glad you didn't," I said.

"I imagined you thought me to be a scoundrel. What I told you is hardly flattering."

It was as far as we got before circumstances pulled us

apart. I had traveled up here to attend a lecture at the free school and had arrived at the last minute. The room was packed. Marie Bregdahl was the speaker. I found a seat at the back next to a thin woman in a navy-blue dress who said: "I've been looking forward to this for more than a fortnight."

"Me too," I said.

I told her I had come from Thyregod, and she said, "Imagine!" She was thrilled that their events could attract people from so far afield.

The audience extended into the hallway. I heard not a word of the lecture. Afterwards there were refreshments. I stuck to the woman in the navy-blue dress and went with her into the kitchen to butter bread. She was the first person I met here and we became friends that same evening. I am talking about Helene. When it was finished, we cleared the things away, and boiled kettles of water in the kitchen for the washing-up. There was chatter and laughter, and I was a part of it; my hands have always been able if ever there was a need.

When eventually the school had emptied and everything was spick and span, the last cup had been returned to its place and even the dishwashers had gone, and after Marie

Bregdahl had drunk a beer and been shown to her bed in the annex, the time was approaching midnight. Erland found me out in the hall.

"I like it here," I said.

"And everyone wants you here," he said.

"How can you tell?"

"They take joy in the joys of others," he said. Written down, those words seem rather instructive, but Erland is not instructive. He took me into his rooms, put the lamp in the window, and his arms around me, and kissed me.

Now the snow is falling over all of Jutland, on Carl Carlsen's beehives, and Inge's and Dagmar's kitchen garden. On Hilda's little house, and Peter Carlsen's windbreaks and orchards. Tomorrow he will go out and inspect his trees, smooth an ungloved hand over an occasional trunk. On Vigand's grave the snow falls too.

That night, when I stood with Erland in the living room here for the very first time, I said: "You should know that it's been such a long time since I was with a man that I'm practically innocent again."

"Then we must make you guilty," he said.

ACKNOWLEDGEMENTS

Thanks to Kirsten Skriver Frandsen.

Thanks to Gudrun Jessen, my mother.

Thanks to the Give District Museum and Local History Archive.

Particular thanks to Christian Tirsgaard.

The quote on page 84 is from Sigurd Rambusch: *Iagttagelser fra Midtjyllands hedeegne 1890-1904* (Observations from the Heathland Tracts of Mid-Jutland 1890-1904).

A. Ankerstrøm's memoirs *Fra Herning og hedelandet* (From Herning and the Heathland) and *Vej og virke* (Work and Vocation) have been an important source of inspiration.

The portrayal of Terkelline Andersen stems largely from the Give District Musuem's Year Book 2010.

The account of Peter Carlsen's tuberculosis is essentially a direct transcript from the personal documents of Thomas Sørensen, used here by kind permission of Villy M. Sørensen. The original Danish text may be accessed at:

www.nørvang-herred.dk/brande/thomas/Thomas Tuberkulose.

The verse on page 157, from a hymn by Thomas Kingo, appears here in a translation by John Irons.

The excerpt from Ibsen's epic poem *Terje Vigen* on page 140 is in John Northam's translation.

Johannes V. Jensen's poem was translated by Martin Aitken, as were the brief lines of a song by Carl Christian Bagger on page 134.

Although *A Change of Time* takes place in Thyregod and its surrounding area, it is a novel and as such bears only incidental relation to real events or people. During its writing, facts have been displaced, making many descriptions appear blurred to those with knowledge of the actual occurrences and states of affairs. It has not been my intention to write a section of the history of the town in which I grew up, though I freely acknowledge the singular allurement of using the name Thyregod.

To Niels